Rashid and the Haupmann Diamond

RASHID AND THE HAUPMANN DIAMOND
by: Hassan Radwan
Illustrations: Stevan Stratford 2002

British Library Cataloguing in Publication Data

Radwan, Hassan
  Rashid and the Haupmann diamond
  1. Diamonds - Juvenile fiction 2. Ethnic relations - Juvenile fiction
  3. Muslims - Great Britain - Juvenile fiction
  4. Friendship - Juvenile fiction 5. Children's stories
  I. Title II. Stratford, Stevan III. Islamic Foundation 823.9'2[J]

ISBN 0-86037-357-6

Published by
The Islamic Foundation, Markfield Conference Centre
Ratby Lane, Markfield, Leicestershire LE67 9SY, United Kingdom
Tel: (01530) 244944 Fax: (01530) 244946
E-mail: i.foundation@islamic-foundation.org.uk

Quran House, PO Box 30611, Nairobi, Kenya

PMB 3193, Kano, Nigeria

Printed by Ashford Colour Press Ltd. UK

"For baby Safa"

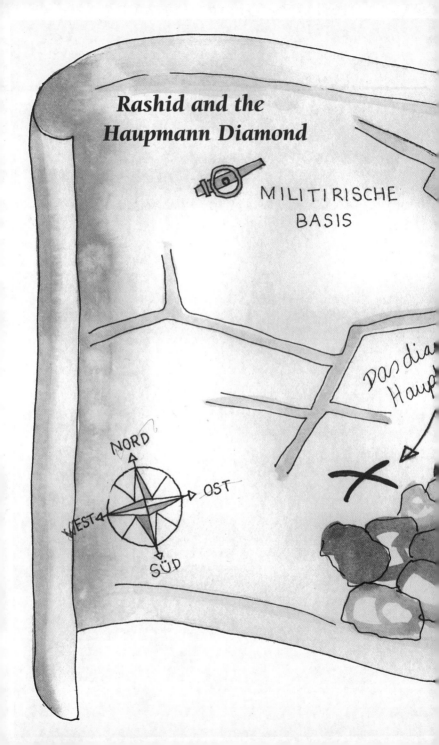

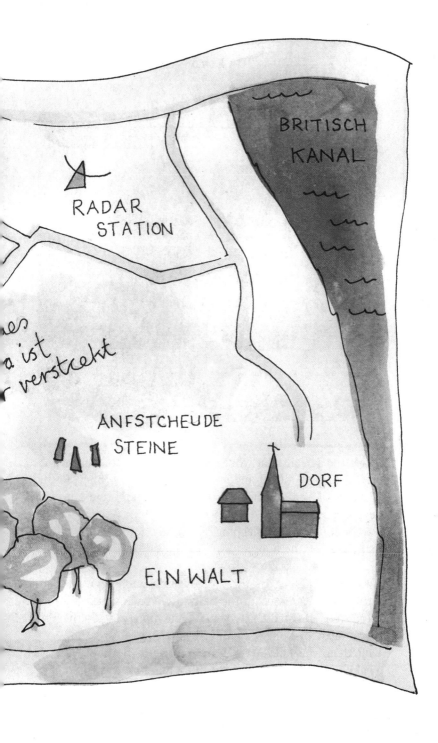

Chapter 1

Sleepover

It was the scream that woke us up. Very faint to begin with, it grew gradually louder and louder. Chris heard it first. "Rashid! Wake up! Listen…," he whispered as he shook me out of my deep sleep.

Gary and Chris were sleeping over at my house. Mum had laid mattresses on the floor and we had stayed up late chatting and planning the next day's activities.

"Oh please, Chris, it's three in the morning!" I groaned as I buried my head beneath the pillow. "Go back to sleep!"

"No listen!" insisted Chris, shaking me more roughly this time. "I can hear someone screaming!"

I lifted up my pillow and leaned forward. By now Gary was awake too and we all listened intently. Chris was right! There was a distant high-pitched scream coming from outside. We listened carefully as it got louder and louder. Then, suddenly, it stopped. As though whoever was making it had been silenced abruptly.

We looked at each other, but before we could say anything we heard another sound; a distant, muffled banging and knocking. It was so faint you could barely hear it.
We crept to the window and scanned the street in silence. Suddenly Chris pointed, "Look over there…" He was trying hard to keep his voice down. It was very dark but we could just about see some dim shadows moving around inside the front room of the house over the road.

"That's Miss Wilson's house," I said. "She lives alone and is never up at this time."
"It must be robbers," whispered Chris, "we should call the police."
"We can't be sure it's robbers," cautioned Gary. "It could be her family or something. Maybe we should go over and check it out."
"But it's the middle of the night!" I said, not sure what scared me the most, coming face to face with robbers or what Dad would say if he caught us going out at this time.
"Well we can't just sit here while someone gets burgled and not do anything about it!" said Chris. And I had to agree.

We slipped on our clothes and sneaked quietly downstairs. It was dark and silent outside and a cold chill ran up my spine. We crept cautiously over to Miss Wilson's front room window and crouched low. "Take a quick look," whispered Gary, as he bent over to keep out of view. I raised my head slowly and peeped inside. Two men were moving about in the room; they seemed to have balaclavas on. I ducked down again, terrified that they would see me and looked at Gary and Chris without saying a word – I didn't have to, my face said it all. After a short pause the three of us lifted our heads slowly and glanced in again. The men had their backs to us. They were opening drawers, looking on shelves and in bags. One of them had turned a desk upside down and was about to examine it closely when he stopped and stood up, perfectly still, as though he had heard something. My heart began to pound and my mouth felt dry. Little by little the man turned slowly around and looked straight over at us!

"Oh no, he's seen us!" cried Gary. We could see him saying something to the other man, then they both moved quickly towards the window.

"RUN!" cried Chris, with terror in his voice. We sprang to our feet, and in our panic fell over each other, stumbling onto the grass. We could hear the men coming out of a window round the back of the house. One of them spotted us.

"There they are!" he snarled gruffly.

Gary slipped on the moist grass, so I grabbed his arm and dragged him forwards. "Come on, quick!" And we sprinted across the road shouting and yelling for Mum and Dad to wake up.

Dad appeared at the top of the stairs as we spilled into the hallway and slammed the door behind us.

"*Subhanallah!* What on earth is going on Rashid?" he asked.

"Quick Dad, phone the police, some robbers were in Miss Wilson's house; we heard a noise and went to investigate and saw them, then they spotted us," I blurted out breathlessly.

Dad rushed downstairs and rang for the police while the three of us peeped cautiously out of the landing window. We couldn't see the men and the road was silent and empty once more.

"Do you think they're hiding somewhere?" asked Chris.

"I reckon they must have had a car parked in the next road or something," replied Gary. "They're probably well away from here by now."

About two minutes after Dad's phone call, we saw the police arrive and walk up to Miss Wilson's front door. We watched as she appeared at the door wearing a white dressing gown. The policemen chatted with her on the doorstep, then disappeared inside. Mum told us to come into the living room.

"That was very foolish of you to go over to Miss Wilson's house in the middle of the night!" said Dad angrily. "You should have woken us up and let adults deal with something like this."

"Sorry Dad," I said, looking and feeling very sheepish.

"Well, *al-hamdulillah,* no harm came to you," said Dad, calmer now. "But think carefully before doing anything like that again."

My sister Sabah had made some hot chocolate and we all sat in the living room and waited. Even my little brother Kalim had woken up and was sitting on Mum's lap, wobbling his loose tooth. He had been playing with it all day. At first he was worried that it wasn't supposed to wobble like that. But I explained to him that it was a 'baby tooth' and that now he was becoming a 'big boy' his adult teeth were starting to push through. He was delighted when he heard this and ran around telling anyone who would listen that he was a grown-up now. He even sat on the wall outside our front door, saying to all the passers by, "I'm a big boy now. I'm going to get an adult tooth. Look!" And he would open his mouth wide and wobble his tooth at them.

Most smiled politely and hurried on their way. But one lady gave him a 50 pence piece and told him that when it comes out he should put the tooth under his pillow, so that the 'Tooth Fairy' could give him some money for it. Of course I told him there was no such thing as the 'Tooth Fairy' but he refused to believe me.

Just then my youngest sister Nur came in and sat down beside me. "So who do you think these people were?" she asked.

"Maybe they were robbers!" I answered.

"Maybe they were murderers!" said Chris.

"Maybe they were spies!" suggested Gary.

"Maybe they were the Tooth Fairies!" exclaimed Kalim quite seriously. Everyone burst out laughing.

"Don't be daft Kalim," I chuckled. "Besides, Miss Wilson doesn't have milk teeth, she's already a grown up."

"Maybe the Tooth Fairy was trying to find this house but got lost!"

"Well then perhaps the Tooth Fairy should carry a street map with her next time!" I laughed.

Suddenly, the doorbell rang and we all jumped.

"It must be the police," said Dad getting up to open the door. He was right. Two tall policemen came in and sat on the sofa. We told them what we'd seen and they listened carefully, making a few notes as the story unfolded.

"Is Miss Wilson alright?" asked Dad.

"Oh yes, she's fine," answered the older of the two policemen. "In fact, she had no idea that anything had happened until we rang her doorbell!"

"Did they take much?" asked Chris.

"Well that's the strange thing boys. You see, nothing seems to have been touched at all!"

"What?" said Gary. We looked at each other. "That doesn't make sense!"

"That's right," continued the policemen, "and we couldn't find any signs of a break in either!" He folded his notebook and got up to leave.

"Well, we'd better get back to the station now," said his colleague. "We will be making further enquiries in the morning." He shook hands with Dad and then turned to us and smiled.

"You did the right thing in phoning us, but next time, don't play detectives, it is very dangerous and you might get hurt."

Just as the police car drove away, another car pulled up outside our house. It was a taxi and I could see my eldest sister Huda and her 14-month-old son Amir inside. 'What are they doing here at this time of night?' I thought to myself. Mum went out to meet them and picked up Amir who was half-asleep. Huda was very upset and looked as if she had been crying. They came in the house and went straight up to Mum's bedroom. I switched off the light in the hall and bolted the front door. As I got to the top of the stairs, Dad came out of the bathroom.

"*Assalamu Alaykum,* son, it's almost time for *Fajr* prayer," he said. "Go and make *wudu* and we will pray together downstairs, *insha' Allah.*"

Dad recited a long *Sura* during the prayer, which was unusual because he usually kept his morning prayer quite short. I could tell something was troubling him. After we finished, he turned to face me.

"I have something to tell you Rashid."

Dad looked serious and I was worried that I was going to get told off for something.

"Huda will be staying with us for a while," Dad went on. "She and Ahmed are having a few problems and so Huda and baby Amir will be staying with us until things get sorted out." He paused. "I'd rather this news didn't get around and I'd appreciate it if you didn't discuss this with Kalim. He is too young to understand. As far as he is concerned, Huda is visiting us for a while which gives us the chance to see more of her new baby."

"Okay, Dad. Is it a serious problem?" I asked. "Can I help?"

"*Masha' Allah,* that's kind of you but no, it's just a little misunderstanding, don't worry."

When I got back to my room, I found Gary and Chris still awake.

"This has turned into quite a night of drama," said Gary.

"It certainly has," I replied.

"Is it always like this at your house Rashid?" chuckled Chris.

"Well tonight's been pretty quiet," I replied with mock

seriousness. "You should see it when things get really busy!" We all laughed.

I got back into bed and tried to sleep, but too many things were swimming around inside my head.

"I don't understand why the police found that nothing had been touched," huffed Chris after a long silence. "How could those men have covered their tracks so well and disappeared so quickly?"

"We should try to talk to Miss Wilson tomorrow," said Gary "and tell her what we saw; perhaps she missed something when she spoke to the police."

"Okay, we will, *insha' Allah*," I said as I tried to stifle a yawn. "But now we'd better try to get some sleep."

"I don't think I can sleep now," said Gary. "What I want to know is who were those masked men and what were they after?"

"And who was screaming?" said Chris. "And why did they stop so suddenly?"

With all of these thoughts in our heads, it was some time before we finally drifted off to sleep.

Chapter 2

The Lady in White

"Assalamu Alaykum, Dad, is it alright if we go over to see Miss Wilson?" I asked as we came down for breakfast the next day.
"Wa Alaykum Assalam. Okay, but don't be too long, your mother and I are going over to Ahmed's house, *insha' Allah,* and I want you to baby-sit Kalim and Amir."
"Okay, Dad," I said as I poured cornflakes into my bowl. 'Oh great,' I thought to myself, 'an afternoon of fun with the gruesome twosome!'
I turned to Gary and Chris. "You know who Miss Wilson is don't you?" They shook their heads.
"Who is she?" asked Gary.
"She's 'The Lady in White'; you must have seen her. That old

13

woman who goes around dressed in old-fashioned clothes, always white, even her shoes and hair."

"Yes! I've seen her! So that's where she lives," said Chris. "People say she's mad. I saw her on the bus the other day. When the driver asked her for her fare she said, 'God will pay for me'." He laughed. "She's senile or mentally ill isn't she?"

"She's definitely got a screw loose," replied Gary. "I've seen her walking up and down the High Street talking to herself and acting like she's the Queen or something; then she suddenly stops and starts shouting at no-one in particular. Some people say she's a witch and that she is talking to evil spirits. The kids are always teasing her and winding her up."

"Well, that's her house," I said. "Her real name is Emily Wilson. My Mum does some shopping for her sometimes and helps her around the house. She's not mad, just a bit 'different' that's all."

"Well my cousin knows her," said Chris. "He told me she looks all white because she's really a ghost!"

Gary and I burst out laughing when he said this. It's difficult to tell when Chris is joking or being serious, because he comes out with some strange ideas sometimes.

"You may laugh," continued Chris, "but he says if you go to Parkwood Cemetery you'll find her grave there, with her name on it and everything."

"What are you talking about Chris?" Gary laughed. "How can she be a ghost?"

"That's what my cousin says," insisted Chris.

"Don't be ignorant," I said. "There are no such things as ghosts, and besides, I've seen her at the Post Office collecting her pension money; now don't tell me ghosts need to collect their pension."

"Well I suppose they may need to buy spirits!" joked Gary.

"And shoes," I added, laughing, "because they've got no souls!"

"That's right," chuckled Gary, "and I suppose she never goes out because she has no body to go with!"

By now, Gary and I were laughing so much we almost fell off our chairs.

14

"Alright you lot, very funny," said Chris, rather annoyed with us.

"Hey Gary! What's a ghost's favourite food?" I asked.

"I don't know," replied Gary.

"I scream!" I laughed.

"Oh this is too much!" said Gary and we laughed so much, tears began to roll down our cheeks.

"Well if you two have quite finished," said Chris, indignantly, "I think we should go and see Miss Wilson now."

"Don't get upset Chris, we're only joking with you," I said, catching up with him.

"I'm not upset," said Chris, sounding very upset indeed.

At the edge of the footpath, Chris hesitated.

"Come on Chris," said Gary, "don't be scared."

"I'm NOT scared," said Chris, "I'm just wondering what she's going to say, that's all."

We crossed the road and went up the garden path to Miss Wilson's house.

It was like the rest of the houses in our street, an old Victorian semi-detached, with an imposing front door and huge brass doorknobs. The only real difference was that this one looked neglected and rundown. The lawn was overgrown and covered in weeds. The paint on the door was peeling and the wood around the window frames was rotten and falling away.

"Go on then," I said, "ring the bell."

"Hey, she's your neighbour, you ring the bell," sniffed Gary.

Chris chuckled. "Are you feeling a bit scared?"

"I pressed the bell but there was no sound. I was just about to knock when the door creaked slowly open, making us jump back. An old wrinkled face peeped out. Miss Wilson's eyelids seemed to be half closed and her hair hung in untidy tangles over her forehead.

"What do you want?" she said sharply.

"Hello, Miss Wilson, it's me, Rashid, you know, Mrs. Ibrahim's son, from over the road."

She disappeared for a few seconds and then re-appeared wearing little round glasses with thick lenses. She stared at each one of us in turn, as we smiled awkwardly, feeling a bit embarrassed. Gary leaned over and whispered, "She's seeing if we're fat enough to eat," and we both giggled.

"Oh yes, hello Rashid," she said finally. "I thought it was those hooligans who ring my bell and then run away. They're always putting rubbish through my letter box and writing rude words on my door."

"No! No!" I said, and suddenly I felt very sorry for this frail and frightened old lady. "We would really like to talk to you about what happened last night – the robbers that were in your house – do you remember?"

"Come in," she said, opening the door just enough for us to squeeze in. The house was dark and dusty, but we could see her clearly in her white flowing dress with its fine lace and sparkling sequins. She wore white gloves and white furry slippers. Her eyes were red but her face was pale and smelt of talcum powder.

"Follow me," she said and led us into the lounge where we sat down on a large, deep sofa. "Would you like a cup of tea?"

"Yes please, Miss Wilson, that would be nice," I said and she walked off muttering to herself.

Gary leaned over to Chris. "What do you think about your ghost now?" he whispered.

"Alright, alright, I knew it was rubbish really," Chris replied.

"She's just a lonely old lady, who's a bit on the weird side. There's no harm in that," I said. "People like to make up stupid things about anyone who's different from them," added Gary.

We looked around the living room. It was the room we had seen last night. The men had been looking through these very drawers and cupboards. But now everything looked so neat and tidy, as if everything was where it should be.

Miss Wilson came back in carrying a tray, which she placed carefully on the coffee table.

"About last night, Miss Wilson," said Gary, moving to the edge of the sofa. "Did you hear or notice anything unusual?"

"No, not at all," she answered sweetly, "I was fast asleep, until the policemen rang the door bell."

"Are you sure there's nothing missing Miss Wilson?" I asked.

"Well my memory is not as good as it used to be," she said as she poured the tea. "But I am pretty sure nothing is missing. Besides, I don't have anything of any real value."

Then she stopped pouring and hesitated. "Well... apart from the antique writing desk, that is." And she stared into the air, with a kind of glazed look on her face. "You know, come to think of it, that is a bit strange..."

"What's strange?" I asked.

"Well, a man came round a couple of weeks ago and wanted to buy that desk from me. He offered me a lot of money – more than it is worth. But I said no. You see, it means more to me than money, it has sentimental value." She picked up an old picture from the mantelpiece. It was of a group of young men, standing by an old fighter aircraft.

"The desk was left to me by a friend of my father. They served in the war together." She held out the picture for me to take. "This is my father, Michael Wilson, with some other members of his squadron. He was a Spitfire pilot during the Battle of Britain. This picture was taken only a short while before he died. They believe his plane crashed into the sea, although they never found his body."

Gary and Chris shuffled up closer to me to get a better look.

"Was that the second world war?" I asked.

"That's right. My father is the one with the goggles in his hand. He had just come back from a mission. What he didn't know when this was taken, was that his squadron was about to be scrambled again and this time he wasn't going to come back. Poor chaps; they were exhausted, but they had to keep flying. They were very short of pilots, you see."

"Which one gave you the desk?" asked Gary.

"Oh, he is not in the picture. His name was Henry Atkinson. He survived the war. In fact, he only died a few weeks ago. I was very sad to hear about his death. He was a good man, always so kind to my mother and me, after my father died. He used to send us money and visit us when I was little. He'd tell me about my father and what a great hero he was. You see, that's why I could never sell the desk."

Miss Wilson fell silent. She stared at the antique desk as if she was in a trance, as though she was listening to some distant voices in her head. Suddenly she stood up and began shouting. "You're a naughty, naughty little girl, a bad girl! Go to your bedroom at once."

Then she sat down and began muttering to herself and straightening out her long white dress as if nothing unusual had happened.

We looked at each other, feeling embarrassed and not knowing what to say.

"Could I have a look at the desk?" I said, trying to get Miss Wilson's attention.

She looked up and smiled, "Yes of course, help yourself my dear."

I opened one drawer and found a pile of old photographs, which I lifted out carefully and studied one by one. They were black and white pictures of a young woman and a man in a smart uniform with a little girl. Some showed the little girl laughing as the man pushed her on the swing, while others showed him carrying her on his back.

"Is that lady you?" I asked, holding up a picture of the woman standing in the garden.

"Oh no, dear," said Miss Wilson. "That's my mother and the young man is my father, may God rest their souls. That's me!" She pointed to the little girl laughing innocently on the swing. "I was only 8 years old when my father died, so I don't remember much about him. But I remember he always called me his little princess, his little Snow White. He would take me out and buy me presents." She reached over and picked up a doll of a princess in a white wedding gown.

"He bought me this." And she hugged it to her chest. "He said I was his pretty little Snow White." She began muttering to herself again, rocking to and fro gently cradling the doll in her arms. Gary looked at me and raised his eyebrows, without saying anything.

Chris was busy examining the desk. "Do you mind if I turn this upside down?" he said, as he peered underneath. I remembered that the men had done the same thing, and guessed what he was up to.

"Not at all," replied Miss Wilson, rather puzzled by the strange request.

Chris examined the base of the desk, but saw nothing unusual. He was about to turn it back over when Gary stood up.

"Wait a minute Chris!" he said as he caught hold of one of the legs. "Look at the metal caps on each leg."

"What about them?" asked Chris.

"One of them hasn't been screwed on fully," said Gary. "It looks as though it has been removed but not replaced properly."

Chris began to twist the metal cap.

"It's very stiff," he complained.

He took out a tissue and wrapped it around the cap, then began to twist again. Slowly the cap began to turn. As it became easier, Chris twisted it with his fingers. Eventually the cap fell off into his hand. We peered at the table leg; it was hollow.

"There's something inside here," said Chris, sticking a finger into the hole, "but I can't get it out."

"Here, use these," said Miss Wilson, handing Chris some tweezers. Chris poked them into the little hole.

"Got it!" he said triumphantly as he gently pulled out what looked like an old scroll. He placed it carefully on the coffee table and opened it out. We all gathered around excitedly, to see what it was.

"It's a map of some sort," said Gary as he leaned over Chris' shoulder.

"But the words aren't in English," I said.

"It's German," said Miss Wilson gazing at the paper intently. "I can't read it, but I recognize a few words. This one means 'a forest' and over there it says 'English Channel'. It's a map of part of the Kent coastline, where my father was shot down."

"Do you think it is a map of where he died?" I asked.

"I don't know what to make of this at all. I wonder why Uncle Henry kept this hidden in there?"

"Maybe the robbers were looking for this map!" said Chris, sending a buzz of excitement around the room.

"But if it is a map of where my father was shot down," said Miss Wilson, puzzled, "then why would it be of interest to robbers?"

We looked carefully at the map. Most of the writing was typewritten, but here and there someone had scribbled some notes in their own handwriting. These words were in German too and were very difficult to see, partly because they had faded badly and partly because the handwriting wasn't clear, as though the person were shaking or moving. It reminded me of the sort of scribble that happens when you try to write something when you are travelling in a bus or car.

"Look over here," said Chris, pointing to the area near the forest, "there is a tiny cross and some words by it."

Miss Wilson held it close. "Mmmm, I'm afraid my eyesight is not that good and with it being German and all that, I really can't make head nor tail of it," she said, rubbing her glasses with a small white cloth.

"We'll have to get it translated," said Gary. "Could we take a photocopy of this map, Miss Wilson? We will return it to you safe and sound, don't worry."

"Oh yes, that's quite all right, after all, I wouldn't have discovered it, if it wasn't for you boys," she answered, smiling pleasantly. So, before going home, we stopped off at the newsagent to make a photocopy of the map.

In the afternoon I had to baby-sit for my little nephew Amir, while Mum and Dad went out to Ahmed's house. "I've left a bottle of milk in the fridge," said Huda as she got in the car beside Mum, "and remember to check every so often to see if he's done a poo!"

I was holding Amir in my arms as we watched them drive away. "Well how am I supposed to check if you've done a poo?" I said smiling at Amir.

"Pooooooo!" repeated Amir.

"Yes: Pooooooo!" I chuckled. He knew a few words like mama, baby, no, and spoon, which he pronounced boon and hot which he pronounced ot. He also knew the word Bab, although we weren't quite sure what Bab meant. Huda said it meant his dad but he also used it to refer to his favourite TV programme, Bob the Builder. My own theory on this is that he thinks 'Bob the Builder' is his dad which is why he calls them both Bab. I hope he discovers the truth soon or he will go to Nursery School telling all his classmates that his dad is Bob the Builder. That could be quite embarrassing. Mind you the other children will probably believe him!

I took him into the lounge where Kalim was watching Adam's World.

"I put this on for Amir," said Kalim, grabbing the baby from me and sitting him on his lap. But Amir didn't want to sit and watch a video and he wriggled to get free.

"Look, there's Adam," said Kalim. "You like Adam, don't you?" he asked as he hugged Amir tightly so he couldn't escape.

"Just let him go Kalim," I said sitting down on the sofa. "If he doesn't want to watch it, then just leave him."

"But I put it on especially for him," said Kalim sounding rather disappointed. "Look, here's my favourite song." And he began to sing: "Take me to the *Ka'ba*, I must go there!"

But Amir just toddled off to the corner of the room where he found something far more interesting… a rubbish bin! He peered inside with gleeful anticipation and reached out to grab the contents. I jumped up as quickly as I could and snatched hold of him. But he had already tipped the bin over and plundered a few trophies – a dirty tissue, an old banana skin and a mouldy bit of bread. When I had finally wrestled them from his iron grip I sat him on my lap, but he soon wriggled free again and toddled off to look for more things to mess around with. After some serious exploration, he found the huge bag of nappies that Huda had left in the corner. "Pooooo!" said Amir as he looked up at me with a cheeky grin to see if I was going to stop him. I decided to let him play with them. I reckoned it was the lesser of several evils. If it kept him quiet, what's the harm? Amir judged my indifference correctly, and set about removing one nappy after another and tossed each one carefully over his shoulder. He was soon almost completely covered by a mountain of nappies.

Kalim, who had been quietly watching the Muppet-clone Adam, suddenly stood up holding his nose. "Eeeeewwww! SOMEONE'S done a stinky doo doo!" he said, pointing in the direction of the pile of nappies.

"Oh no," I groaned as I picked up Amir and pulled back his nappy to look for the evidence. Sure enough, his bottom was covered with the biggest and smelliest poo I had ever seen.

"Great! It's only been 5 minutes and in that time he's already managed to spill a rubbish bin, empty a bag containing 100 nappies and do a giant poo," I complained to no one in particular, while laying him flat on the changing mat. "Oh boy, this is going to be a really fun afternoon."

"He's only a baby Rashid," said Kalim, who came over to give me a hand with changing him. "He's not a grown up like you and me."

"Ha!" I laughed, "you're not a grown up, you're still a little kid!"

"No I'm not!" said Kalim indignantly as he held out a plastic bag. "I'm an adult now. I've got an adult tooth!" And he opened his mouth wide and wobbled his wobbly tooth.

"I can't see anything," I snapped, glancing quickly at his mouth.

"That's because it hasn't come out properly yet, but it is there. I can feel it," said Kalim sticking his fingers in his mouth.

I picked up Amir, who was nice and clean now, and I threw him gently into the air which made him chuckle with delight. So I did it again. Which made him laugh louder. So I did it again and again, which made him laugh louder and louder. I loved it when Amir laughed. He would throw his head back and his whole face would light up as he chuckled wildly making his body vibrate with ecstasy. It was that infectious carefree and joyful laugh of a child that makes you want to laugh too. Kalim, who was jumping up and down on the sofa started to laugh as well and soon all three of us were laughing our heads off. 'Baby-sitting is not so bad after all,' I thought to myself, still laughing.

Chapter 3

The Battle of Britain

Early the next morning I felt something cold drip onto my face. I opened my eyes and saw Kalim standing over me with a glass of water, laughing mischievously. Another drop fell on my cheek.

"Shall I?" he chuckled.

"You dare!" I shouted, covering my face with my hands.

Kalim gently tipped the glass.

"I mean it Kalim, if one more drop falls on me, you're dead meat!"

Kalim continued to tip the glass until the water had reached right up to the rim. Then he stopped and grinned, daring me to move, which would of course make the water spill.

I lay still, but glared menacingly at him.

Kalim could hardly contain his laughter and snorted through his nose. But this made his hand tremble and the ice-cold water rippled slowly over the rim and down on to my face.

"Right, that's it, you're dead!" I said jumping up.

"No, no, no… sorry Rashid!" shrieked Kalim as he ran out the door, "I didn't mean to spill it! It was an accident." I chased him along the corridor and he disappeared into Mum and Dad's bedroom. I stopped short of the door, knocked, made *Salam* and waited for Mum's sleepy reply before following him inside. He had dived into bed with them. I stood at the doorway as he peeped out from under the covers.

Kalim had started to sleep in Mum and Dad's room again. It started after he saw a documentary called Alien Abduction. It was about aliens who kidnap people from their rooms and take them to their own planet to study. Kalim was convinced that aliens were trying to sneak into his bedroom at night to kidnap him. He had become so frightened that he would not sleep in his own room any more.

I got dressed and came downstairs for breakfast. Kalim was already sitting next to Dad, who was drinking coffee and reading the paper.

"*Assalamu Alaykum* everybody," I said. Then I turned to Kalim, "Don't worry Kalim, I'll get you," I grinned. "You can't hide behind Mum and Dad all day!"

"Dad," whimpered Kalim, "Rashid is going to hit me."

"Don't hit your brother, Rashid," said Dad glancing up from his paper.

I just smiled menacingly at Kalim who was leaning his head on Dad's arm and sucking his thumb.

I decided it was a good idea to read up a little on 'The Battle of Britain' as it might help us to solve the mystery of the map. So I got a few books on the subject from the local library and settled down in the front room and began to read. I was soon absorbed by the events of World War Two and became increasingly fascinated by the old fighter planes. While I was trying to read, Kalim played in front of me, attempting to stand upside down on his head, but he kept falling into my lap.

"Can't you go and play outside?" I asked roughly as I pushed him off for what seemed like the zillionth time.

"I can't," he said, pausing to look nervously out the window, "they're out there!"

"Who's out there?" I asked.

"The aliens!" he whispered. "They're waiting for me to go outside so they can grab me!"

"Right... that's it!"

I slammed my book down on the table and grabbed Kalim by the arm. "We are going into the garden and I will prove to you that there are no aliens!"

Kalim started screaming and kicking. I was just pushing him through the door when Mum came downstairs.

"*Subhanallah!* What on earth is going on?"

I loosened my grip on Kalim and he darted back into the living room.

"I was just taking him out into the garden to prove that there are no aliens!"

But before Mum could respond, the phone rang.

"Hi Rashid."

It was Gary.

"I've just had an idea. Why don't we take the map to Mr. Watkins, the Head of Modern Languages? He teaches German to Years 10 and 11."

"That's a great idea," I replied, "but how are we going to explain it? I mean, we don't want the whole school finding out about our map."

"Don't worry," replied Gary. "We can tell him that it's a special assignment we have to do. That's called being economical with the truth, I think!"

"Okay, it sounds good. As long as we don't have to lie. See you in school tomorrow."

So after school the next day we went to Mr. Watkins' room and showed him the map.

"We were hoping you could help us translate it," said Gary.

Mr. Watkins put on his spectacles and scrutinized the map silently.

"Well, well," he muttered under his breath, "very interesting!" He turned it over to check the other side then turned it back again and scanned the words as we watched with eager anticipation.

"It looks like a navigation map of some sort," he said suddenly. "Possibly of the type used during the Second World War."

He held the map up to the light and squinted.

"It's certainly a map of the Kent coastline. Over here it says '*Radar Station*' and here it says '*Military Base*'. I suppose these were the targets. The rest of the names are mainly just local towns and villages."

"What does this say?" I asked, pointing to the words next to the tiny cross near the woods.

"Hmmmm… quite fascinating!"

He looked up at us and smiled, "It says, '*The Haupmann Diamond is hidden here*' – whatever does that mean?"

He handed the map to Chris.

"The Haupmann Diamond!" said Chris excitedly. "Have you ever heard of such a thing sir?"

"No, I can't say I have, Christopher. This must be a very special assignment…"

"Er… thank you sir," said Chris as he folded up the map, catching Mr. Watkins mid-sentence and heading for the door before the teacher could ask any more questions. "Thanks sir," we chorused as we left his room rather too hurriedly.

We headed home with only one thing on our minds: *The Haupmann Diamond!*

"A diamond!" I gasped once we had cleared the school gates. "It could be worth, thousands… or millions!"

"We're going to be rich and famous!" said Chris.

"Er… sorry to spoil your dreams guys, but aren't we forgetting something?" said Gary. "Even if we find the diamond, it doesn't belong to us. It probably belongs to Miss Wilson's friend, Henry Atkinson, or it may even be stolen."

"Or it might not even be there," I added.

"Well the first thing we need to do is to find out if there is really such a thing as 'The Haupmann Diamond' and learn a bit about it!"

"How can we do that?"

"On the Internet of course, you can get information on just about every subject you can think of," said Gary. "Come on over to my house and we can search the web on my computer."

When we got to Gary's house his dad was in the kitchen standing over a saucepan that was boiling furiously. He was wearing an apron that said, "I'm not a complete idiot – several parts are missing!"

"Hello Mr. Jacobs," said Chris and I together.

"Ah! Hello boys, come in, come in," he replied, waving to us. "You are just in time to taste my latest creation, I call it chicken surprise."

"Why 'chicken surprise'?" I asked, peering cautiously into the pan.

"I'm glad you asked me that Rashid! You see it doesn't have any chicken – that's the surprise!"

"Well what's in it then?" asked Gary.

"Tofu! – it's a sort of meat substitute, it's very tasty, here try some." And he held out a spoonful. We looked at each other and waited for someone to volunteer to have a taste.

"No meat you say?" I asked, not wishing to be rude.

"No meat at all," said Mr. Jacobs with a big smile on his face. "No fat, no oil, no salt, no chemicals, no additives."

"And no taste!" whispered Gary in my ear.

I looked at Mr. Jacobs holding out the spoon towards us, and thought that I ought to do the decent thing and taste it. I took the spoonful into my mouth. It was horrible! It tasted like water and cardboard. I wanted to spit it out, but instead I smiled and gulped it down. "Mmm! Interesting taste," I spluttered diplomatically.

"Oh wonderful Rashid, I'm so glad you like it! Here, let me put some on a plate for you, you can have it with my special rice!" I was about to ask why it was called 'special rice' when Mr. Jacobs held out the pan, saying, "The special thing about it is that it is not rice at all! It's cracked wheat! Much healthier than rice, with lots more roughage."

I was trying hard to think of a good excuse that wouldn't sound too rude, when Gary saved me.

"We've had lunch Dad so we're not really hungry right now," he said, "perhaps later."

"Okee dokee boys – no problemo!" said Mr. Jacobs as we dashed upstairs. "I'll save you some."

"Great!" whispered Gary as we entered his room.

After starting up his computer and connecting to the Internet, Gary typed in the words 'Haupmann Diamond' and clicked SEARCH. The screen went blank then flashed back with a huge list of links and their brief descriptions.

"This one looks interesting," said Gary as he clicked a link. A title page came up saying "History Zone – Flying Aces".

I peered over Gary's shoulder as he read the text below.

"Baron Von Haupmann was a German Ace during the First World War."

"What's an ace?" asked Chris.

"It means a pilot who has shot down many enemy planes," I said, feeling very pleased with myself that I had read up on the subject.

Gary continued, "The Haupmann Diamond was an extremely large and very valuable diamond that had been in the Haupmann family for generations. It was believed to bring 'good luck' to whoever possessed it. Baron Von Haupmann always took it with him when he flew into battle and when he retired from service he passed it to his son, Heinrich, who was a bomber pilot during World War Two. Heinrich kept it in a gold pendant, which he wore around his neck, whenever he flew. However, the diamond was lost when Heinrich was shot down, by a Spitfire, over the Kent coast. Although he'd managed to bail out and was captured, the diamond was never found. Its whereabouts is still a mystery today!"

Gary looked up from the screen and smiled at us.

"Well perhaps its whereabouts will not be a mystery for much longer," he said, sitting back in his chair.

"So you reckon this was Heinrich Haupmann's map?" asked Chris. "And it shows where he hid his diamond?"

"Well that's what it would seem to be," said Gary hesitantly.

"That's a bit of a coincidence," I said.

"What is?" said Chris.

"That bit about Heinrich being shot down by a Spitfire, over the Kent coast. I mean, you don't think that the Spitfire pilot could have been Miss Wilson's dad, do you?"

"Well we can try and find out," said Gary. "They used to keep records of who got shot down and where and so on." Gary scratched his head. "What shall I type into the search engine?"

"Let me have a go Gary," I said, nudging Gary off the chair. "Let's try… 'Battle of Britain'." I clicked SEARCH.

To our surprise there were hundreds of links, although most of them were of no use. We scrolled down the page and eventually found what we were looking for. I began to read.

"On September 23rd a Squadron of Spitfires was scrambled to intercept a convoy of German bombers heading towards Kent. The Spitfires intercepted them as they reached the south coast… In the ensuing battle nine Heinkel bombers were shot down…"

I scanned through the names of the pilots.

"Ah here it is!" I said excitedly. *"The Spitfire pilot who shot down Heinrich's plane was…"* – I paused to look up at Chris and Gary – "Michael Wilson!" I said triumphantly. "It says that Heinrich bailed out safely and then Michael himself was shot down."

"Does it say what happened to him?" asked Chris. "Did he bail out too?"

"It says there was no clear account about what happened to him," I replied. "One report says he and his plane plunged into the sea, but this was unconfirmed."

"What about Henry Atkinson – is he mentioned at all?" said Gary. "After all, he was the one who had the map."

I typed in 'Henry Atkinson' and searched several times but didn't find anything. I sat back.

"Perhaps Heinrich lost the diamond when he bailed out," said Chris.

"Yes, and what if Michael Wilson didn't die?" I said sitting up. "He might have found the diamond and hidden it and then given the map to his friend, Henry Atkinson!"

"But if Michael Wilson didn't die," said Gary, "then what happened to him? Why didn't he come home to his wife and daughter, Emily, I mean Miss Wilson?"

We all fell silent. It was certainly quite a puzzle.

A few days later, we were walking along the High Road, on the way home from school, when we saw Miss Wilson up ahead. A group of boys were throwing stones at her and teasing her. She was dressed all in white as usual and wearing a white bonnet with a large white ribbon. She looked confused and spilled some of her shopping on the pavement. The boys just laughed as she began talking to herself out loud. There were many people around, but no one stopped to give her a hand.

"Come on!" I said as we rushed over to help her.

"Get lost and leave her alone!" shouted Gary to the boys as we stooped to pick up Miss Wilson's shopping. One of the boys shouted something rude and then they ran off laughing. Miss Wilson looked very agitated. She was shuffling her feet up and down and slapping her cheek.

"You go straight to bed my girl!" she said to herself. "No supper for you tonight!" Then she started singing an old song quietly. It took us quite a while to calm her down.

"Are you alright Miss Wilson?" I asked, taking hold of a bag of shopping for her.

"Oh yes, my dear, quite alright," she smiled. It was as if nothing had happened.

As we walked home we told her what we had discovered so far about the map. She listened quietly, not saying a word, until suddenly she stood still and looked at me.

"Is father going to come home now?" she asked. "He's been gone an awfully long time."

I didn't know what to say and looked to Gary and Chris for help.

"We'll do our best to find him," said Gary.

We walked on quietly until we reached her front door.

"Thank you my dears," said Miss Wilson as she opened her front door.

I carried the shopping to the kitchen as she picked up some letters from the mat.

"Oh dear," she said as she looked up from one of the envelopes, "another letter from the council."

"Is there a problem?" I asked.

"Well, you see I've been having trouble paying the rent," she replied, looking agitated again, "and the council wants me to move out of this house and into a Special Home. They say that I can't look after myself."

"Don't worry Miss Wilson, we won't let them put you in a home," said Chris gallantly; and he meant it. We all did.

"And when we get the diamond, you can use it to buy this house," I added, "then they can never throw you out."

She smiled a little and put the letter on the sideboard along with a pile of others, many of them unopened.

"I was wondering," I said, stepping forward, "if you could tell us any more about Henry Atkinson, the one who gave you the table. It may help us find the diamond for you. Was he a pilot like your father? We can't seem to find any information about him."

"I'm afraid I really don't know much about him," replied Miss Wilson. "He was a very private man. I know he was a pilot, because he sometimes talked about how he loved flying. But he hardly ever mentioned the war. I never thought about it at the time, but now it does seem rather odd that he never talked about himself."

She paused for a moment.

"Hang on a minute!" she said and went into the living room. She came out again clutching an old photograph.

"This is the only picture I have of him. It was taken after the war."

She handed it to me and I studied it careful. There was some writing on the back. It said *'Love and Best Wishes from Henry'*. The writing was scribbled and shaky. I had the feeling that I had seen this handwriting somewhere before.

Chapter 4

Prisoners of War

We propped our bikes up on the small bridge that arched over Dollis Brook and sat dangling our feet over the side. We had been playing 'Cops and Robbers' and were now exhausted after chasing each other all round the park. We sat staring at the water as it rushed over pebbles, through gaps between the rocks, and wound it's way out of sight. We had no idea where it was going or where it started. We tried to find out once. We had followed it far along its course in both directions. Crossing over roads and following it through endless parks and common land. But we had discovered neither it's source nor it's end.

"Look at this!" said Gary pointing to a mass of ants crawling in a long line along the edge of the brook. We got down on our stomachs to get a closer look and watched in silence as the ants marched in a long line. Occasionally they would meet more ants coming in the opposite direction and would stop, briefly, to touch antennae and then march on. It was as though they were speaking to each other. I wondered what they were saying. Were they reporting what they had seen further down the brook? Or were they perhaps passing on orders from the Queen ant? Chris kneeled down beside us and, with a stick, he cut a deep trench across the path of the marching ants. Water quickly filled the artificial canal, blocking the ants' advance. We watched silently, wondering what they would do next. At first the ants looked confused and milled back and forth, touching antennae at every opportunity. Eventually a few ventured further along the canal until they found a place to cross. But instead of continuing, they returned to the others, as if they wanted to tell them what they had discovered. Soon all of them were following the new route across the tiny canal. Then off they went, marching purposefully onwards along the bank.

"That's amazing!" said Chris as we sat up. "They are so clever, it's like they're all working together, with each one knowing what its job is."

As we watched the ants I remembered something I had read.

"There is no creature on earth nor in the sky, but forms communities like you!" I recited.

"Where did you hear that?" asked Chris.

"That's from the Qur'an," I answered.

"Amazing!" replied Gary as he smiled and pulled me up on to my feet.

"Oh my leg's gone stiff!" cried Chris hobbling towards his bike.

"You know I bought that game 'Air Combat' the other day," said Gary as we pushed our bikes down the path.

"Really? What's it like?" I said.

"It's brilliant, you must come over and have a go!" he said

excitedly. "And I've joined 'SimHQ.com', it's a sort of Internet discussion board where people can talk about the game or stuff to do with aircraft."

"What's so interesting about that?" asked Chris. "Just a bunch of nerds talking about flight simulators."

"Well they may be nerds, but they certainly know a lot of things about aircraft and World War Two," said Gary defensively. "I asked them if anyone had heard of the names Michael Wilson or Heinrich Haupmann and I got quite a few replies, basically telling me what I already knew. But then yesterday I got a very interesting email from this guy who calls himself 'Flying Tiger'."

"Okay, come on then, what did he say?" I asked eagerly.

"Well, he told me that he read an article a few years ago about German prisoners of war. He said the article explained that when the war ended and the German prisoners were released, some never returned to Germany. They decided to stay in England and become British Citizens. For example there was one famous German prisoner of war who became a goalkeeper for Manchester City in the 1950s."

"Yes, I've heard of him, his name was Bert Trautmann," I said. "He's the one who broke his neck in the 1956 FA cup final."

"That's right," continued Gary, "but 'Flying Tiger' told me that he remembers the name Heinrich Haupmann from the article."

"What does he mean?" I said. This was getting interesting.

"He means that Heinrich Haupmann was one of the German prisoners of war who never returned to Germany," replied Gary. "He stayed here and became a British citizen!"

"So that means he could still be here!" I said excitedly. "Maybe we could find out where he lives and go and see him."

"That's what I thought, so I e-mailed back to Flying Tiger and asked him if he could get any more information about what happened to Heinrich Haupmann. He seemed really pleased to help and said he would do some research and get back to me."

"Excellent," I said. "I'll pop over tomorrow and we can see if he's replied."

The next day I was sitting in the lounge when Kalim came in, followed by little Amir, who was clutching an armful of teddy bears and bunny rabbits. Amir had started following Kalim wherever he went. He also copied everything Kalim did. For some reason little babies seem to love other children. Maybe they recognize the same childish spirit, or maybe they like the fact that they are small like themselves. Kalim took the teddy bears and rabbits from Amir and arranged them in a neat circle around him. Then he sat Amir down in front and picked up a big children's book called ABC and he began to read. Amir sat very quietly listening with all his attention towards Kalim. I couldn't understand how Kalim got him to do that. Amir would never sit still with me for a second.

Kalim began to read: "BIG A… little a… What begins with A?" I watched carefully wondering what he would do next. I knew Kalim couldn't really read and he had only learnt the first few lines of that book by heart. So I watched to see how he would read the rest of it.

"Alligator begins with A!" he said, and flicked the page over as Amir gazed admiringly at him.

"Baby has a haircut… begins with B" continued Kalim.

'Here he goes,' I thought to myself, 'he's just making it up now!'

"Camel upside down… begins with C," he said.

"It doesn't say that!" I interrupted, and went over to look at the book. "Look!" I said pointing to the words: "It says, 'Camel on the ceiling…'"

"I'm not reading the words," protested Kalim, "I'm reading the pictures!"

"You are not supposed to read the pictures you Muppet!" I said laughing at him.

"Yes you are!" replied Kalim adamantly.

"Well if you are supposed to read the pictures, then why do they put words there?" I said.

"The words are there for people who can't read the pictures!" answered Kalim, confidently. I couldn't really think of an answer to that one, so I just gave up. By now Amir had grabbed the little bunny rabbit sitting next to him and was sucking its toes. I decided it was time to leave.

"*Assalamu Alaykum,* Mum, I'm going to Gary's house," I called up the stairs. "I won't be long, *insha' Allah.*"

"Alright," answered Mum. "But I'll be going out with the children later, *insha' Allah,* so I may not be in when you get back. *Fee Aman Allah!*"

When I got to Gary's house, I found him and Chris at his computer, reading e-mails.

"Hi Rashid," said Gary. "Look, we got a reply from 'Flying Tiger'."

"Well come on, read it!" said Chris impatiently.

Gary double clicked on the e-mail and began to read.

"Hello Eagle Eye!"

"Who's Eagle Eye?" I laughed.

"Oh that's my nickname on the Forum," said Gary. "We all have nicknames."

Chris and I looked at each other and laughed out loud.

"OK Eagle Eye! Carry on reading…" I said, still chuckling.

Gary went on: "This is what I have been able to find out. Heinrich Haupmann and his observer were able to bail out, but only Heinrich was captured. His observer was never found. Heinrich was taken to Ridgley Prisoner of War Camp in Lancashire, where he was held for 5 years until the war ended. On release he applied for residency and eventually became a British Citizen. He married a local woman, Nelly Atkinson, and lived in Rochdale for most of his life. He spent the last few years in the Summerdale Nursing Home, where he died on May 25th this year, at the age of 85."

"That's only six weeks ago; what a shame, if only we had known all this a few weeks ago we could have met him before he died," said Chris.

"Yes," I said, "I'm sure he held the key to this mystery."

Gary looked thoughtful: "Funny that, isn't it? About his wife's name I mean."

"What's funny?" I asked.

"Well, I mean her name being Atkinson, the same as Miss Wilson's friend, Henry Atkinson."

"That is a bit of a coincidence," I said.

"And not just that," said Chris, "both Henry Atkinson and Heinrich Haupmann died six weeks ago."

"You don't think someone is bumping them off?" said Gary. "I mean killing anyone who had anything to do with the diamond?"

"It's possible," I replied. "If only we could find out more information about Henry and Heinrich!"

"They even sound similar!" laughed Gary.

"What do you mean, they sound similar?" I asked.

"I mean the names, Henry and Heinrich," replied Gary. "They sound similar, don't they?"

"Now that you mention it," I said, repeating the names in my mind, "I suppose they do."

"Can't you e-mail your friend Flying Tiger and ask him where he got his information from?" said Chris.

"Yes, sure," answered Gary and he began tapping away on the keyboard.

"I'd better be going now," I said getting up to leave.

"Okay Rashid," said Gary. "Oh, and don't forget you're coming over to watch the game on Sunday."

"How could I forget? COME ON YOU SPURS!" I shouted as I went down the stairs. Gary had satellite television and they were going to show the FA cup semi-final, Tottenham v Arsenal, so we had arranged to watch the game together, *insha' Allah,* because we are all fans of Tottenham Hotspur Football Club, the Kings of North London!

When I got home the house appeared to be quiet and empty. Mum and Dad had gone out with Kalim and Amir. But as I passed Nur's room, I heard someone crying. I knocked, made *Salam,* and went inside where I found Nur and Sabah with their arms around Huda, who was sobbing gently with her head in her hands.

"What do you want?" asked Nur looking up sharply.

"I heard the crying," I replied sitting down by Huda's side.

"What's the matter Huda? Is there a problem with Ahmed?" I asked. Huda looked up, her eyes were red. But she didn't say anything.

"Yes, there is a problem with Ahmed," answered Nur, "just like all men." And she gave me a disdainful sideways glance.

"Don't be like that Nur," said Sabah as she patted me on the leg. Out of all my sisters, I think I was closest to Sabah. She always took the time to explain things to me and treated me like an adult, unlike Nur, who was always sarcastic and argumentative.

"It's rather complicated Rashid," Sabah went on. "It's just that Ahmed and Huda look at life slightly differently."

"What do you mean, 'slightly differently'?" I asked.

"Oh it's useless explaining anything to him!" said Nur angrily. "He won't understand and even if he does he will probably take Ahmed's side anyway."

But Sabah ignored Nur and continued. "You see, Ahmed wasn't born and brought up in this country as we were. Where he comes from men sometimes have a different attitude towards their wives."

"But doesn't he come from a Muslim country?"

"Yes he does, but there are many customs and practices in Muslim countries that sometimes have nothing to do with Islam. In fact, in some cases, they are against the teachings of Islam. But many Muslims don't realize this."

"Okay, but how does this affect Huda and Ahmed?" I asked.

"Well, Ahmed tends to go and buy things for the home without consulting Huda, even quite big things, like furniture. He thinks he is doing her a favour and giving her nice surprises when, really, she'd much rather that they chose things together, as a couple." Sabah paused... "The problem is that they have been arguing a lot recently over this and other things have come into it. Now the arguments have become quite serious."

"Would you like me to talk to Ahmed?" I asked as Huda started crying again.

"Oh don't be silly Rashid, you're only a child!" said Nur. I was angry when she said this.

"*Jazakallah,* Rashid," said Sabah. "But I think we had better leave this to our parents and Ahmed's parents." And she smiled. "Don't worry, everything is going to be sorted out, *insha' Allah.*"

I gave Huda a hug.

"Don't cry Huda, Allah will help you, you'll see," I said trying to comfort her. Huda looked at me and smiled.

On Sunday I went over to Gary's house as arranged for the big match. His dad answered the door wearing a Tottenham scarf and a navy-blue and white bobble hat. He had one of those noisy kids' trumpets in his mouth.

"Hello Mr. Jacobs," I said as I stepped in. But Mr. Jacobs didn't answer, he just blew the trumpet and pointed to his T-shirt slogan which read, 'Beep if you love Spurs'.

"Er... beep, beep!" I said, at which a beaming Mr. Jacobs gave me the thumbs up. I went into the living room where I found Gary and Chris already watching the pre-match build up.

"Hi guys," I said, handing Gary a carrier bag containing some samosas and chicken dippers.

"Hi Rashid," smiled Gary as he took the bag. "Samosas, cool, but you shouldn't have bothered. We have plenty of stuff," and he pointed to the coffee table, which was covered with plates of peanuts and crisps, slices of home-made pizza, fresh bagels and cartons of orange juice. I sat down next to Chris and helped myself to a few crisps. Suddenly Mr. Jacobs came in with a drum around his neck. He was banging it and singing, "Come on you Spurs!" very, er, enthusiastically. Then he began marching around the coffee table: "Come on you Spurs!" was followed by a blast on the trumpet as he marched out of the room.

"Oh, and don't worry about my Dad," whispered Gary, "he's not staying; he's going over to the Leiberman's next door, with Mum."

"I don't mind Gary," I laughed, "I think your dad is funny."

We settled down to watch the match and were soon jumping for joy when Spurs scored the first goal. The match ended in a 3–0 victory. Yes!

"I can't believe we made it to the final!" gasped Chris, "I wish I could get tickets."

"I'm just glad we beat the Gunners," I said, "as far as I'm concerned that's as good as winning the Cup!"

We all cheered in raucous approval but our cheers were drowned out by loud singing from outside. We looked out of the window and there, coming across the lawn, was Gary's dad and two of his friends from next door doing what appeared to be the 'conga' up the garden path, singing, *"We're going to win the cup, we're going to win the cup, ee ay adio, we're going to win the cup… "*

"Oh no," cried Gary in despair, "they're coming in here!"

I could see he was embarrassed and so I tried not to laugh, but when Chris started laughing, I just couldn't help it.

"Quick, let's run upstairs to my room," pleaded Gary as the 'Dancing Daddies' neared the patio door.

"Don't worry Chris," I said sitting up on the sofa, "I wish my dad was as much fun as yours!"

Suddenly the door was flung open and in they came.

"YES!" shouted Mr. Jacobs. "We did it!" He waltzed over to give us some high fives.

"These are Gary's school chums," said Mr. Jacobs taking off his cap and placing it carefully next to the fine porcelain figurines on the mantelpiece. "This is Rashid and that's Chris," he smiled. "Anyone for a celebratory drink of my finest, homemade Guava and Apricot cocktail?"

"Er, not for me, thanks Mr. Jacobs," I said.

The two men from next door shook hands with us.

"My name's Henry," said the short man with black curly hair. "Where are you from Rashid?"

'Oh no – here we go again,' I thought to myself. I hate having to answer that question all the time. People usually only ask it because my name is Rashid or because of my colour.

"I'm from here," I replied. "Just down the road by Meadow Park."

I could see he was a little confused.

"But my parents came from Pakistan," I added quickly.

"Ahhh!" he said, as it suddenly dawned on him. "I'm sorry I don't mean to be nosey." He smiled and sat down on the sofa. "Actually my parents came from abroad too."

"Where from?" I asked casually.

"Germany," he answered. "My mother and father fled in 1939 when the war broke out."

I remembered what I had read about World War Two and how Hitler had persecuted the Jews, and anyone else who didn't fit in with his plans for a so-called master race. The lucky ones had been able to escape, but millions had been rounded up and exterminated in concentration camps.

"Did all of your family manage to escape?" I asked.

"No, I'm afraid not. My uncle Heinrich and his family were arrested and murdered by the Nazis."

"I'm very sorry to hear that sir."

"When I was born my father named me Henry in honour of my uncle."

I sat bolt upright. Suddenly this was very interesting. "Did you say he named you after your uncle Heinrich?"

"Yes, that's right," replied Henry.

"But your name is Henry, not Heinrich," I said.

"It's the same name. Henry is simply the English form of Heinrich."

"OF COURSE IT IS!" I shouted jumping to my feet.

"Are you alright?" asked Henry, looking very startled.

"Yes, thank you, I'm fine," I smiled as I looked over to Chris and Gary. "Let's go upstairs guys, we need to talk."

We excused ourselves very abruptly and rushed upstairs to Gary's bedroom.

"What's the matter Rashid?" asked Gary as he shut the door behind us.

"That's it!" I declared. "That's it! It has been staring us right in the face but we were too stupid to see it!"

"What's been staring us right in the face?" asked Gary, clearly feeling rather inadequate.

"It's obvious: Henry Atkinson and Heinrich Haupmann are – were – one and the same person!" I declared excitedly. "I should have known. There were too many similarities for them to be coincidences. They died at the same time. Heinrich had married a woman called Nelly Atkinson, the same surname as Henry Atkinson. Then there was the scribbled handwriting we saw on the back of Henry Atkinson's photo – I knew I had seen that before… it's the same handwriting on the map."

I was triumphant: "Heinrich Haupmann's map!"

"Shhhhh! Gary's dad will wonder what's going on up here," said Chris peeping out of the door. But we could hear Mr. Jacobs and his friends singing another football song.

"Then again, perhaps not," he chuckled.

"Once we know," I said, "that the names Heinrich and Henry are the same name, it doesn't take a genius to realize that Henry Atkinson and Heinrich Haupmann were really the same person!"

"It's incredible," said Chris. "You mean all this time Henry Atkinson pretended to be a friend of Miss Wilson's father, when he was really a German pilot?"

"And not just any German pilot," I added, "but the pilot of the very plane that Michael Wilson shot down."

"But… if Henry was really Heinrich all the time," said Chris, "then that means he must have had the diamond."

"Then why did he pretend to be Michael's friend and why did

he leave Miss Wilson the table with the map in it when he died?" I said, very puzzled. "He must have known that the map would be discovered eventually."

"Let's see if Flying Tiger has sent me any more info," I said.
Gary switched on the computer. There were several e-mails in his "Inbox" including one from 'Flying Tiger'. He opened it immediately and read it out aloud.
"Hi Eagle Eye. You wanted to know where I got the information about Heinrich? Well most of it I got from Arthur Hughes, who is a resident at Summerdale Nursing Home where Heinrich spent his last years. Mr. Hughes was Heinrich's best friend during his time there. If you contact him, I'm sure he can tell you more. Best wishes and good hunting! Over and out. FT."

"Well if anyone knows Heinrich's secrets, his best friend will," I said.
"We must go and talk to him," said Gary.
"I'm going up to Manchester soon with my family. We're going to visit my cousins for *Eid al-Adha,*" I said. "I'm not sure where that nursing home is, but if it's somewhere in Lancashire, then it might not be too far from Manchester and I could go and talk to Arthur Hughes."
"That's a great idea Rashid. Give them a ring from here and find out where it is," said Gary.
We got the number of the Summerdale Nursing Home from 'Directory Inquiries' and when the phone was answered I asked if I could speak to Arthur Hughes. I explained who I was and why I was ringing. When he came on the line, Mr. Hughes seemed very nervous when I mentioned the name Heinrich Haupmann and said that he did not want to talk on the phone. So I asked him if I could try to visit him and he said yes, of course.
"Okay, Mr. Hughes, bye for now," I said, putting the phone down. "That's odd."

"What is?" asked Gary.

"You know that sound you get when there is someone else on the phone?"

"You mean like when I answer the phone downstairs and my sister picks up the extension upstairs?" said Chris.

"Yes, like that," I replied. "It sounds different and you can almost 'feel' another person listening on the line."

"Yes, yes, so what is your point?" said Gary irritably.

"Well, while I was speaking to Mr. Hughes, it sounded just like that."

"Do you mean there was someone else listening to your conversation?"

"Yes, and I could tell that even Mr. Hughes knew it because he didn't want to talk. He sounded very nervous."

"That's scary," said Chris. "I wonder who was listening?"

"Be careful when you go up there Rashid," said Gary, "I have a feeling that we are not the only ones who know about the diamond."

Chapter 5

Old Secrets

Auntie Aysha and Uncle Saeed stood by the front door as we pulled up in the car. Their *au pair* came out to give us a hand with our bags.

"That's okay," I told her as she offered to carry my bag. "I'll carry it."

But she didn't seem to understand and kept trying to take the bag from me. Kalim, who was standing next to me, leaned over and whispered in my ear.

"She's Pork and Cheese!"

"Wh... what...?" I stammered. "What... are you talking about?"

"That's why she can't understand you. Mum told me that she's Pork and Cheese and she only speaks Pork and Cheese."

"You nitwit," I laughed. "You mean, Portuguese!" I couldn't stop laughing. "You didn't actually think there was a country called 'Pork and Cheese' did you?"

"Well that's what it sounded like to me," said Kalim as he marched off.

The *au pair's* name was Maria and she had come to Britain to learn English. So Kalim decided that he was going to teach her. I told Mum and Dad that this was not a good idea, especially since Kalim could hardly speak English himself. But they seemed to think it would encourage him to be responsible. Being responsible and grown up was the latest 'thing' with Kalim. His wobbly tooth had finally come out and he was now convinced he was an adult and no one could tell him otherwise. What made it worse was that little Amir thought Kalim was an adult too! He looked up to Kalim and followed him everywhere and copied everything he did. For the next few days we were treated to the hilarious sight of Kalim, a little 5 year old, acting as if he was a university professor and marching around with Maria and little Amir hanging eagerly on to his every word. Kalim went around the house pointing out the name of everything on the way. What made it worse was that he kept trying to tell them the spellings of all the words he was teaching them. He had already told them that 'house' was spelt H-O-W-S and that 'school' was spelt S-K-E-W-L!

"This is called a sandwich," said Kalim as Maria and Amir looked on. Kalim spread a thick layer of jam over an equally thick layer of butter, not forgetting to spill huge lumps all over the kitchen table. "Now you spell sandwich, S-A-N-D... er," and he paused to wipe his sticky fingers on his shirt. "W-I-J," he concluded. "It's called a sandwich because in olden times they used to use sand instead of jam."

'Now he's just making it up,' I thought to myself.

"And this is called juice, spelt J-O-O-S."

Poor Maria! She's going to return to Portugal totally confused, I thought, as Kalim marched off towards the living room, followed by his faithful attendants.

We woke up early on *Eid* day and put on our best clothes to go to the mosque. My elder cousin Sohaib came down looking very smart in his white *Jalabeyya* and a white cap on his head. "Here Rashid," he said holding out a small bottle of perfumed oil. "It's Musk, the Prophet's favourite scent, *Sallallahu Alayhi wa Sallam.*"

"Jazakallah," I said, placing a small amount on my right hand. Maria was coming with us to the mosque, so she could help Mum with the children.

"We'll have to take both cars," said Uncle Saeed to Dad. "There are too many of us to get into one."

I went with Dad and Sohaib, while Kalim sat between Maria and Amir at the back.

"This is called a mosque," announced Kalim, as we found a place to park. We had told him that Maria was a Christian and therefore possibly didn't know much about Islam so he had gallantly decided that not only would he teach her English, but he would also teach her about Islam!

"A Mosque is a bit like a church but with Muslims inside instead of Christians," he told Maria confidently, who responded with a polite smile.

"We are going to say our prayers now. I'm going to ask Allah if I can have a Party Penguin – Ice Lolly Maker."

I groaned and buried my head in my hands, deciding not to get involved. It would only make things worse.

"Would you like me to ask Allah if He will get you an *Eid* present too? I'm sure He's got plenty."

Even Dad couldn't help laughing at that one.

"Eid is not about getting presents," said Sohaib sternly. "It's about giving thanks to Allah."

"Well that's okay then," replied Kalim, "because I haven't got you a present."

Mum and Auntie Aysha met us in the courtyard and took Maria, Amir and Kalim with them to the ladies' section, much to Dad's relief.

I had already phoned the Nursing Home and arranged to meet Mr. Hughes on Thursday, the day after *Eid*, around lunchtime. When I got there a nurse led me to a large dormitory where I saw an old man sitting in a wheelchair. He was all alone by the window, gazing out across the rolling Lancashire countryside.

"Mr. Hughes?" I asked rather timidly.

He turned slowly and smiled.

"Please call me Arthur," he replied in a friendly tone. "You must be Rashid."

"Yes, that's right. I must say that I'm really grateful that you agreed to see me, Mr. Hughes, especially since you don't really know me or anything."

I couldn't bring myself to address him as "Arthur"; he was older than my Grandad and the Prophet, peace be upon him, told us to show respect for our elders.

"I've come to talk to you about your friend, Heinrich Haupmann."

Mr. Hughes looked around nervously.

"I think it would be best if you could take me out for a little walk, so that we can be alone," he said as he leaned forward to release the brake on his wheelchair. "I don't want anyone to hear what I have to say."

I took hold of the handles of the wheelchair and guided him through the double doors leading to the garden. We followed a long winding path that made its way through the woods at the far end of the Nursing Home grounds.

"You are Miss Wilson's neighbour I believe," he said finally when we were a good distance from the home.

"That's right, my friends and I are trying to help her solve the mystery of an old map we found at her house."

"Well if you're a friend of Miss Wilson then I know I can trust you," he said, still looking around anxiously.

"It's alright Mr. Hughes, there is nothing to worry about," I said trying to reassure him.

"Oh yes there is my boy! Oh yes there is."

The way he said those words made me feel really on edge. I found myself looking around suspiciously for signs of any intruders.

"Did you know Heinrich Haupmann well?" I asked.

"Yes, but he never told many people that was his real name. Most folk round here knew him as Henry Atkinson. He came here after his wife passed away, about 2 years ago. He was a wonderful old fellow, very warm and generous. It didn't take us long to become very good friends; we were inseparable. He used to take me out for walks, just like you are now, and we would just walk and talk. Eventually he told me his secret; that his real name was Heinrich Haupmann and that he had been a German pilot during the war."

"Did he tell you about Michael Wilson?" I asked.

"Oh yes. He described the day he was shot down by Michael's Spitfire. He said that after he bailed out he saw Michael's plane crash land near some woods. Then when Heinrich's parachute set down, he ran over to see if he could rescue Michael, but found him trapped and fatally injured in the mangled wreckage of his Spitfire."

"But if he was a German pilot, why did he go over to rescue Michael?" I said feeling confused.

"War can be a strange thing Rashid," replied Arthur. "People kill each other because they're told to, not because they hate each other. Many Germans didn't really understand why they were being ordered to attack and bomb Britain. It was their leaders who were the evil ones. The ordinary people were just like you and me. Under different circumstances, Heinrich and Michael could have been good friends."

"I see," I replied, "so Heinrich tried to save Michael?"

"Yes, but Michael knew he was dying so he took a picture of his wife and daughter out of his pocket and scribbled a message to them on the back. He asked Heinrich to pass it on to them and make sure they were alright. Heinrich promised he would do all he could for them. Then Michael passed out and died. Heinrich felt that this was his chance to do something good. He remembered that he still had the diamond round his neck, so he decided to give it to Michael's wife and child."

"But how could he do that?" I interrupted. "Surely he would have known that all his possessions would be taken from him if and when he was taken prisoner?"

"Exactly! So he put the diamond in Michael's pocket, thinking that when someone discovered the wrecked plane and Michael's body, all his possessions would be passed on to his family."

"But Michael's Spitfire was never found, was it?" I asked.

"No, but Heinrich was duly caught and taken to a Prison of War camp. He was afraid to say anything about Michael in case he was blamed for his death. So he marked the location of the Spitfire on his map, hoping that he would one day get the chance to pass it on to Michael's family. By this time, after the war, he had married a local girl, Nelly Atkinson, and had changed his name to Henry Atkinson. He started his own business and very few people knew about his past. He wanted to keep it that way, so he said nothing to anyone but he kept his promise to Michael and went to visit his wife and daughter, Mary, telling them that he was an old war friend. He always made sure they were alright."

"But why didn't he give them the map?" I asked, enthralled.

"Well he couldn't do that without revealing his true identity. He was afraid that it would cause problems for him and his new family, so he hid the map in his old writing desk and had his Will made out to make sure that it would be sent to Michael's daughter, Emily Wilson, when he died."

"I see," I said scratching my head. "What a story! To think that he managed to keep all that a secret for all those years."

"Well yes, almost. After we became friends he told me, but the problem was…", he paused to look around again, very nervously, "…that someone overheard us talking."

"Who was it?"

"A nurse who used to work here. His name is Nick Grimes, a real sneaky character, always prying into the residents' personal business. He's a real gold-digger, always on the lookout for ways of making money. He overheard us talking and found out about the diamond. After that he started asking questions, trying to find out where it was hidden. He knew about the map and the writing table. When Heinrich died, Grimes left the nursing home suddenly."

"Do you think he could have been one of the men who broke into Miss Wilson's house to try and steal the map?" I asked.

"Possibly. Or more likely he hired some people to burgle her house for him. He's the sort that gets others to do his dirty work and some of his cronies still work here. I'd watch out if I were you. Be very careful. If he knows you have the map, then he'll be after you. He is a dangerous and evil man."

Mr. Hughes looked around again nervously, and I shared his anxiety.

"Perhaps we'd better get back," I said.

I pushed him up the path and back to the Nursing Home. I thanked him for all his help.

"Be careful Rashid!" he said as I waved goodbye and went to get the bus back to Manchester.

"I will!" I shouted back. "And thank you again for your help!"

Chapter 6

Screams in the Night

The morning after we got home from Manchester I woke early and was walking past Kalim's room when, to my surprise, I saw him saying his prayers. Mum and Dad had told him that if he says all his prayers on time, then Allah will protect him and won't let any aliens sneak into his room. They did this to try to get him to sleep in his own room and stop him getting into bed with them, and it seemed to be working. Not only did he sleep in his own room now but he had started saying all his prayers on time too, *masha' Allah*.

"So you're not afraid of space aliens any more then?" I asked Kalim.
"No, because Allah is guarding my room all night," he said

smiling from cheek to cheek. "Allah never sleeps, you know, and He's very strong, even stronger than Dad! So the aliens are too scared to come into my room now that He's guarding it."

He looked thoughtful for a second, then said, "But I suppose they might try to get into your room Rashid."

I am sure that I detected a note of concern for my welfare!

"Oh don't worry," I said, "Allah is guarding my room too, *Al-hamdulillah.*"

"But how can He guard both our rooms at the same time?" asked Kalim. "Does He keep going from my room to yours and then back again?"

"No," I laughed, "Allah is not like us. He doesn't have to walk between your room and mine. He can see us both at the same time. He can see everything. He is The God of all the worlds!"

"Can He see all the murderers and bad people?" said Kalim.

"Yes," I answered.

"Then why doesn't He just catch them all and put them in prison?" he asked earnestly.

"Hmmm, that's a tricky one," I replied. "I think it's because Allah lets people do what they want. He wants people to choose to be good by themselves, without forcing them."

Kalim fell silent. I'm not sure he understood. But at least I had shut him up for a while.

I phoned Gary and Chris after breakfast. They were both eager to come over and hear what I had found out. When they arrived, I told them how Heinrich Haupmann had hidden the diamond in Michael Wilson's Spitfire. I also told them about the nurse, Nick Grimes, who had overheard Heinrich and was now after the diamond.

"Well what are we waiting for?" asked Chris excitedly. "Let's go down to Kent and get the diamond, before this Nick Grimes gets his hands on it!"

"There's no need to panic," I replied. "Don't forget, we've got the map so there's no way Nick Grimes will be able to find the diamond without it."

"Well I'm not so sure about that Rashid," said Gary. "If he knows we've got the map, then he'll try and get it from us any way he can." He frowned.

"He's right!" exclaimed Chris, turning to me. "He's already hired some thugs to break into Miss Wilson's house; who knows what he might do next to get that map?"

"I think we'd better be on our guard Rashid. Perhaps we should take turns in looking after the map."

"Okay, that's not a bad idea," I agreed. "And it's also time we went over to Miss Wilson's to tell her what we've found out and make sure she keeps her copy of the map well hidden."

"Half-term is coming up soon," said Gary as we crossed the road to see Miss Wilson. "Why don't we go down to Kent then? What do you think, Rashid?"

"Okay, we could go up there for the day," I replied. "It wouldn't take us very long by train."

After we had told Miss Wilson everything we had discovered and advised her to keep her map well hidden, I began to wonder if Nick Grimes had already been watching us. The thought of being followed and spied on made me feel very uncomfortable.

"Would you like to sleep over at my house tonight?" I suggested as we walked back across the road. "I'm sure Mum and Dad won't mind, and that way we can all keep an eye on the map."

"That's a great idea," said Chris, who was, I think, feeling as nervous as I was.

"Okay Rashid," agreed Gary.

That night I lay in bed, thinking about the things Mr. Hughes had told me. I wondered if Nick Grimes was outside right now, watching our house from behind a lamp-post. I imagined him with the collar of his raincoat pulled up and his hat down low over his face to hide his identity, like shady characters do in detective movies. I wondered if he had a gun strapped to his body, or whether his hired thugs were sitting in a car nearby waiting to grab us if we went outside. It was some time before I dozed off to sleep.

Suddenly, I found myself in the cockpit of a Spitfire, drifting quietly over an endless white landscape of clouds below me. The only sound was the engine, purring gently as my aircraft swayed gracefully up and down in the clear blue sky. Then, without warning, I heard the dull thud and clink of bullets hitting metal and I was thrown forward, hitting my head on the dashboard. In an instant the aircraft went into a steep dive through the clouds. Thick, black smoke poured from my engine as I glanced over my shoulder and caught a glimpse of a German fighter plane sending another burst of machine-gun fire towards me before wheeling away in the blinding bright sunshine. I pulled the joystick back feverishly, desperate to pull out of the spiralling dive, but a strange weakness overcame me and I felt suddenly cold and clammy. I could feel my clothes damp with blood and I realized that I had been hit in the side.

The Spitfire continued its death plunge through the clouds. All I could see were wisps of white fog whistling by my cockpit. Every now and again it would clear momentarily so that I could see the green and brown patchwork of fields and farmland as I hurtled helplessly towards the ground. I struggled desperately with the catch to release the glass canopy so that I could bail out, but the flames had made the metal rivets around it red-hot. Every time I tried to pull it back my fingers were burnt. I tried to cry out in pain, but no sound would come out. The ground got closer and closer. Now the roads and farmhouses were clearly visible. Closer and closer. Again I tried to cry out, but barely any sound came out. Closer and closer… then everything went black.

I sat up suddenly in bed. I had been dreaming. But I could still hear a faint screaming in my ears. I looked over to Chris and

Gary. The screaming continued. Chris stirred and opened his eyes. Gary also woke up. Now the screaming was louder.

"Can you hear it?" I whispered, confused and a little breathless.

"Yes, that's the same scream I heard the other night," said Chris scrambling out of bed.

We went over to the window and looked out across the street to Miss Wilson's house. Suddenly the scream stopped. Just as it had done several nights before.

"I can't see anything moving," said Gary. "Do you think we should go across and see what it is."

"Hang on a sec, look over there." Chris was pointing down to the right. "There's somebody coming out of the house next door."

"That's Brenda the night nurse," I said. "She always goes to work at this time."

I opened the window and almost hissed her name, trying to be quiet and loud enough at the same time.

"Brenda!"

She looked up at my window. "Hello Rashid," she said in a whisper. "What are you doing up at this time?"

"We thought we heard screaming and we think someone may be in trouble. Did you hear anything?"

She looked thoughtful for a second or two, then smiled.

"Mmmm! I think I know what that sound was."

She went back inside the house. A moment later we heard the screaming sound again. It started off very faint then got louder and louder. Then it stopped suddenly. Brenda came out again.

"Was that the noise you heard?" she asked.

"Yes," I said.

"I'm sorry Rashid, but that is my new alarm clock. It makes an awful noise and recently I have been sleeping with my window open, which is probably why you were able to hear it. I'll see if I can replace it."

"That's okay, Brenda," I said feeling a bit silly but also relieved that it wasn't really someone screaming.

I closed the window and got back into bed.

"Of course, how foolish of us!" said Gary. "That night when Chris woke up, it wasn't someone screaming at all. It was just your neighbour's stupid alarm clock!"

"Well it was a good thing it did wake me up," answered Chris. "Otherwise we would never have discovered the robbers in Miss Wilson's house, would we?"

"Come on guys let's get back to sleep. We've had enough sleepless nights to last a lifetime!" I said as I jumped back into bed and pulled the blanket over my head.

I woke early the next morning, but was too tired to get out of bed. I lay there with my eyes shut, trying hard to fall back to sleep, but it was useless. Then I heard little feet plodding down the corridor. I opened my eyes just in time to see Amir toddle quickly past my door. He had pulled Nur's *hijab* over his head, so that only one eye was visible and he was carrying her handbag in one hand and a bottle of perfume in the other. He was heading for the bathroom. 'Oh no!' I thought, 'I'd better get him quick!'

His latest little game was throwing things into the toilet. I don't know why he found that such fun. Maybe because we never allowed him to go near it by himself, or maybe it was that he wasn't allowed to play with water. I don't know what it is about human nature, we seem to be more interested in the things we are not allowed to do rather than the things we are. As soon as Amir felt that no one was watching him, he would toddle off as quickly as his little legs could carry him and head straight for the toilet. I knew I had to be quick if I was to prevent Nur's handbag and perfume disappearing down the pan!

I jumped out of bed, raced down the corridor and grabbed him just as he was lifting up the toilet seat. He let out a cry and kicked his legs, as if to say, 'How dare you!'

"What's going on?" shouted Mum.

"I just caught Amir going to the toilet again," I replied.

"Oh Nur!" said Mum as she came up the stairs. "You were supposed to be watching him!"

Nur came running out of her room with a towel around her head.

"I am, I am! I was just drying my hair. He's so quick, I didn't realize he was gone!"

I laughed. And despite being upset, so did Mum.

On the way to school, Chris kept looking behind us.

"Do you think we are being followed?" I asked.

"Yes I do," replied Chris. "I mean Nick Grimes knows we've got the map and so either he or one of his friends will be watching us."

"Do you have the map with you Rashid?" whispered Gary over my shoulder.

"Yes, I carry it with me all the time."

"Do you think that's wise?" he asked. "I mean Nick Grimes might try to mug us. He's already broken into a house to get the map. Who knows what he'll do next?"

"Well... maybe. But I just feel safer when I've got the map with me."

"I've got a secret compartment in my bag," said Chris. "We could keep the map in there and no one will be able to find it."

"Okay," I said, and carefully passed him the map. We stopped while he put it away and fastened the bag again.

As we walked down the road I felt certain that we were being watched. A tingly sensation came all over me and I could feel the hairs on the back of my neck stand up. I stopped and looked around.

"What's the matter Rashid?" asked Chris.

"I don't know for sure," I replied, "but something doesn't feel right."

We looked about us. There were several people around: a man buying a newspaper a few yards away, a woman looking in a shop window and a group of people standing at a bus stop.

Over the road there was an elderly man sitting on a bench and two people sitting in a car. It could be any one of these people who was watching us, or it could be none of them. I looked up to a window of a house nearby and I saw the curtain fall, as if someone had been looking out.

"Come on Rashid," said Gary. We walked on, but I couldn't get rid of the feeling that someone was watching us.

Chapter 7

Monkey Business

At school we met our new Biology teacher, Mr. Radcliffe. He brought in a life-size human skeleton and began our lesson by asking us to name and explain the functions of the various bones. When describing the spinal column he mentioned that it ended in a short protrusion, which some believe is the remains of a tail and shows how humans evolved from other animals, such as apes.

"Excuse me, sir, but that is not a proven fact is it?" I said feeling very nervous about speaking up in the middle of the class. "I mean, there are many people who do not accept that humans came from apes."

Ian Boyle, who was the class bully, shouted out from the back, "Well not in your case Rashid, because you're still a monkey!"

The class began to laugh.

"That's quite enough of your rudeness," said Mr. Radcliffe firmly, "and get your feet off the table." Then he turned to me. "Yes there are certainly many people who do not accept this. Are you a Muslim, Rashid?" he asked.

"Yes I am sir and we don't believe that humans came from apes."

"But how do Muslims explain all the scientific evidence such as bones and skulls, that seem to prove that humans did evolve from apes?"

"Well God knows best how He makes each creature. But it seems to me that when you have a set of bones, it is either an ape or a human," I said turning bright red and feeling as if I was under a spotlight.

"Well you are certainly entitled to your opinion, Rashid," he said with a smile. "Thanks for bringing it up. In science we should consider all the available evidence carefully. Perhaps we can discuss this again, I always enjoy a good debate."

At break time we were playing football when Sanjay kicked the ball high over the fence. We saw the ball bounce round to the back of the school.

"I'll get it," I said as I dashed through the gate and round the corner. Behind the bike sheds I found Ian Boyle and his mates smoking cigarettes.

"What are you staring at Monkey Boy?" shouted Boyle as I picked up the ball.

"Nothing," I replied, as calmly as I could.

"Yeah, well you'd better not tell on us, or you'll be sorry!" he sneered.

"I don't care if you want to kill yourself by smoking," I snapped and took the ball back to the playground, but the whistle for 'in time' went almost as soon as I returned. As we lined up to go into school, Mr. Jobson called out the bully's name. He said he had been seen smoking behind the sheds and had to go to the headmaster's office immediately. Boyle looked over at me angrily.

"I'm gonna get you at home time Monkey Boy!"

I wanted to let him know that I hadn't told on him, but I thought, 'what's the use, he wouldn't listen to me anyway.' I spent the rest of the day feeling very tense and fearful about what Boyle the bully was going to do to me. Normally I look forward to hearing the bell for home time, but this time, when it rang, it made me jump with fright. Gary leaned over and whispered.

"Listen Rashid, why don't we sneak out the back way? That way Boyle and his gang won't see us."

"No way!" I answered. "Then I'd have to spend the whole night worrying about him beating me up tomorrow. No, I've got to get this over with now."

Gary and Chris came with me as I walked towards the school gates. We saw Boyle and his mates standing outside. The word had somehow got around school that there was going to be a fight, so a large crowd had gathered to watch. Everyone was chanting... "Fight! Fight! Fight! Fight!..."

My stomach turned and my legs began to shake. But I did my best to look calm and brave as I walked right up to them.

Boyle threw down his bag and sneered.

"Okay Monkey Boy, this is where I beat your head in!"

But as he raised his fists, Mr. Radcliffe appeared suddenly from behind the crowd.

"What's going on here?" he shouted, looking at the large crowd. One of the children shouted: "Ian Boyle's gonna beat up Rashid for telling on him, sir!"

"Come here Boyle!" said Mr. Radcliffe angrily. The bully swaggered slowly up to Mr. Radcliffe.

"Look up there, can you see my Biology Lab?" the teacher asked.

"Yes," snapped Boyle insolently.

"Well in case you didn't notice, it looks directly over the bike sheds. I've been watching you all week. It was me who saw you smoking and it was me who told the headmaster." Then he leaned up close to Boyle's face and said, "Do you have a problem with that?"

Boyle looked down at the ground and mumbled.

"No."

"Pardon me Boyle," said Mr. Radcliffe, "I didn't quite hear you."

"No sir!" said Boyle a bit louder.

Some of the children started to giggle.

"Go home Boyle," said Mr. Radcliffe. "Now! Before I put you on a week's detention."

Ian Boyle picked up his bag and marched off grumbling under his breath. The crowd soon dispersed and I was left standing there with Gary and Chris.

"Thanks Mr. Radcliffe," I said.

"That's okay Rashid," he smiled. "You know sometimes I'm not so sure that we humans really are much better than the apes."

We all laughed.

On our way home we stopped off at the newsagent. While I was looking through Spurs Monthly I became aware of another customer in the shop. I glanced quickly to my right. A tall, thin man was standing a couple of yards away flicking through the pages of a gardening magazine. Somehow I got the feeling that this man was not interested in gardening at all. Every now and then he glanced at us through the corner of his eyes. It was him, I was sure of it, the man who had been following us and watching our every move. I shuffled closer to Gary and nudged him in his ribs.

"Ow... what?" said Gary, sounding rather irritated. I didn't say anything, but just raised my eyebrows and rolled my eyes towards the man. Gary leaned forward slightly and peered at him, then he looked at me but didn't say a word. I knew he understood. He went over to Chris who was reading The Beano.

"Come on Chris let's go," he said pulling his jacket.

"Hang on a minute," protested Chris, "I haven't finished."

"Let's go NOW," insisted Gary and he rolled his eyes towards the man who was now flicking through a cookery book. Chris realized what we were trying to say to him and he put the comic back on the shelf and followed us out of the shop. And, just as we had expected, the tall, thin man left the shop too and began following us. We quickened our pace and dodged in and out of the pedestrians along the busy High Road. But the man just quickened his pace too. We couldn't lose him.

"I know a short cut to my house," I said. "Down Woodhouse Road and across the abandoned railway line."

"Okay let's go," answered Gary.

We took a sharp turn left and dashed down a narrow alleyway that led to the bridge across the railway line. Stopping for a while up on the bridge we looked back along the way we had just come. We couldn't see anyone and were just about to congratulate ourselves that we had lost him, when we saw the tall, thin figure appear at the head of the alleyway. He stopped for a second and looked up to the bridge where we were standing, then began to run quickly. We all turned and ran as fast as we could down the steps, jumping down the last few. I fell over and grazed my knee, but Gary helped me to my feet and we sped across the car park and down the road as fast as we could. We could hear the man coming down the steps behind us.

"He's catching up with us!" shouted Chris. "What are we going to do?"

We looked around desperately thinking of a way to escape. The man was now running at full speed down the road.

"Let's knock on someone's door," said Gary and we ran up to a house and began knocking and pressing the bell wildly. But nobody answered. The man was getting closer and closer. He would catch up to us in seconds. We didn't know what to do. Suddenly we saw a car coming. We jumped over the fence and ran into the road in front of the car and began waving our hands in the air for it to stop.

"Help! Help!" we all shouted. The car's brakes screeched as it skidded to a stop, only inches from our legs. We threw the doors open and jumped in quickly.

"There's a man chasing us!" yelled Chris pointing to the man behind us, who had now stopped running. "He is trying to mug us!"

"Calm down boys," said one of the men in the car as he turned towards us and grinned. "Calm down, there's no need for all this fuss."

Suddenly I felt a cold chill run down my spine. I recognized that voice. It was the same gruff voice I had heard outside Miss Wilson's house, that night we saw the robbers. Suddenly we heard the 'click' of the central locking, sealing us in the back of the car, as the man laughed. We struggled with the doors, but it was no use, we were trapped. The tall, thin man, who had now reached the car, leaned over to the driver's window panting and puffing heavily.

"What took you so long?" he asked the driver. "I told you to head them off as they came over the railway bridge!"

"I tried to, Nick! But they were too quick for me."

The driver opened the back door for the two men to get in, squeezing us between them.

"Well, well, we meet at last boys," said Nick Grimes, still gasping for breath. "You gave me quite a run for my money."

He laughed and then began coughing. The driver backed up the car and turned right, heading towards the abandoned railway line.

"So you're Nick Grimes," I said. "And these must be the men who tried to rob Miss Wilson's house I presume."

"Well you don't get any prizes for guessing that," scoffed Grimes. "Now listen boys, I don't have time for any nonsense, just give me the map and you can go."

"We don't have it any more," I said. "We gave it to the police."

"Nice try Rashid, nice try," laughed Grimes. "But I overheard you tell the others that you always carry it with you!" And he began searching through my pockets. When he didn't find the map he began searching the others.

"Okay, enough games," he said angrily as he shoved Gary back onto the car seat. "Now tell me where the map is, or things could get pretty nasty; do you understand me?"

He squeezed my neck.

"We haven't got it!" said Gary adamantly.

Grimes looked at Gary. Then he looked at Chris who was hugging his bag. "You're keeping very quiet young man," he said. "Tell me… are you hiding something in your bag?"

"No, nothing… just school books," Chris said, too anxiously.

"Mmmm! Well if you don't mind, I'll just take a quick look." And he snatched the bag from Chris' grasp, threw the school books out and searched it carefully.

"Ahhh! What's this? A secret compartment?" And he chuckled. "Let's have a look."

He unzipped the small pouch sewn into the lining of the bag and slipped his hand inside. Then he screwed up his face in anger and flung the bag back into Chris' face.

"Nothing there!" he growled.

I gave Gary a puzzled look. The map should have been in Chris' bag. It didn't make sense.

"Come on Nick, we're wasting our time with these kids," said one of the men as he looked around nervously.

"Okay," replied Grimes, sounding very frustrated, "You may be right."

We heard the 'click' of the central locking again and Grimes opened the door and pushed us out onto the ground, along with Chris' bag and books.

"This isn't over yet!" he shouted out of the window as the car screeched off and disappeared round the corner.

"Hey, what happened to the map?" I asked, as we helped Chris pick up his stuff. "I thought it was hidden in the secret compartment of your bag."

Chris laughed. "When we were on the bridge and I saw Grimes coming down the alleyway after us, I was worried that he might catch us," he replied. "So I dropped the map off the bridge onto the embankment."

"Well done Chris, you're not as stupid as you look!" I said cheekily.

"Good thing too," laughed Gary, "because he looks pretty stupid!"

"Ve-ry fun-ny… But if it wasn't for me, we wouldn't have the map any more."

"Well, let's go and see if it is still there," I said running off towards the bridge.

We climbed through a gap in the fence and on to the embankment and began searching amongst the overgrown weeds and grass.

"Here it is!" smiled Chris as he bent over to pick up the map.

"Excellent," I said. "Now this time we'd better make sure we keep it well hidden."

I tucked the map into my top pocket. We decided to walk home along the embankment because it went right past my back garden. We felt sure that Nick Grimes and his associates would not be able to follow us there.

When we got home we told Mum what had happened and she phoned the police. Unfortunately none of us had noted the number or even the type of car that the men had been driving. But we did give the police a good description of the men. Especially Nick Grimes, who was, apparently already a wanted man. The police said that he was a petty thief and was wanted in connection with several thefts at the Old People's Homes across the country where he had worked as a Nursing Assistant. After the police left, Gary and Chris went home.

"Don't forget to hide that map well," said Gary as he left. I went to my bedroom, thinking of the best place to hide the map. Eventually I decided to put it in the middle of an old book called The World Atlas of Mysteries and placed it on the top shelf. I felt sure that no one would be able to find it there, *insha' Allah.*

I went back down to the living room and saw Kalim playing with Amir on the carpet. They were both crawling around and making silly noises. Every now and again Amir would give Kalim his bottle of milk, which Kalim slurped like a baby. Then Amir would chuckle and snatch it back again. I decided to leave the two babies to their silly games and went into the kitchen to get a drink. Suddenly Kalim came running in crying loudly and rubbing his head.

"What's the matter?" I asked, but Kalim could hardly speak through his tears. Eventually he wailed, "Amir pulled my hair!"

"It's alright Kalim, it's alright," I said rubbing his head. "Amir is just a baby; he doesn't realise that pulling hair hurts," I said trying to comfort him.

It seemed to work and Kalim soon calmed down and went back into the living room. But a few seconds later I heard some more crying. This time it was little Amir screaming loudly. I ran into the room and picked him up.

"What happened?" I shouted as Amir continued to scream and cry loudly.

"I was just showing him that pulling hair hurts," said Kalim innocently. "Now he knows!"

"Oh Kalim, you silly boy, you shouldn't have done that!" I said angrily.

"I just wanted to teach him that's all!" whined Kalim.

"Astaghfirullah, that's not how you teach a baby," I replied.

"Well I can't tell him," said Kalim, "because he doesn't understand grown-up talk, he only speaks baby talk."

"Oh Kalim!" I said in exasperation as I gently rocked Amir until he had calmed down. "How would you like it if I smacked you, to show you how much smacking hurts?"

"But there's no reason to do that," answered Kalim, "because I already know that smacking hurts."

'Perhaps it might not be a bad idea if I reminded him', I thought to myself.

The next day I came back from school with Gary and Chris. We found Miss Wilson sitting with Mum on the sofa looking through the family album. Mum had been out shopping with her and had invited her to come over for tea. Miss Wilson was wearing a large white evening dress with fake pearls dotted all over it. I was beginning to get used to her choice of clothes and no longer found it unusual.

"Hello Miss Wilson," I smiled.

"Hello Rashid," she replied, "we've been looking at pictures of you when you were a baby. You looked so cute!"

'Oh no!' I thought to myself, 'not the baby pictures again!' Mum loved showing everyone pictures of the family when we were babies. It was so embarrassing.

Mum turned the page, "Ahhh here is a lovely one of Rashid at feeding time," she said pointing to a picture of me with porridge smudged all over my face.

"And here is one of Rashid at bath time!" she chuckled.

"Er… Mum, can Gary and Chris stay to tea?" I asked, trying to draw their attention away from the baby pictures.

"Oh yes of course dear," she replied, looking up from the album. "Could you turn the oven off for me please."

"Is your gas back on?" interrupted Miss Wilson suddenly. "The man who came about the gas leak this morning didn't switch mine back on."

"What gas leak?" asked Mum.

"The man from the gas company who came this morning said there was a gas leak in our street and so he had to check all the houses," said Miss Wilson. "He went all round my house."

"No gas man came to our house," said Mum sounding rather puzzled, "and I'm quite sure there was no gas leak in the street."

"Did you ask to see his ID card Miss Wilson?" I enquired.

"Well no, I didn't like to," replied Miss Wilson.

"What about his van? Did it say 'Gas Board' or have some sort of logo?" said Gary as we all began to feel very suspicious.

"Actually I thought that was rather unusual," replied Miss Wilson. "He didn't come in a van at all, he arrived in a car."

"I don't think that he was a gas man Miss Wilson. I think that may have been Nick Grimes or one of his men," I said. "They must have wanted to search your house again for the map."

"Oh dear," said Miss Wilson, holding her hand over her mouth. "Oh dear, oh dear! A burglar in my house and I let him in and allowed him to roam all around."

We went back with Miss Wilson to her house to see if the map was still there. She went straight to a picture of her mother and her as a baby that stood on the mantelpiece and turned it over. "Here it is," she smiled, slipping the map out from behind the picture frame. "Safe and sound."

"Well that's a relief," said Chris.

"Could I take a look at that picture please Miss Wilson?" I asked as I caught a glimpse of some writing on the back. I read the inscription. It said, *"To my dear wife Elizabeth and my daughter Emily – Love you always! Michael."*

"Where did you get this picture from?" I asked.

"Oh, Henry gave that to us after the war. He said that my father had given it to him to pass on, if anything happened to him."

"That must be the picture he gave Heinrich," I said, "when he went over to his Spitfire to try to help him."

Miss Wilson held the picture up and gazed at the words on the back. Then she smiled a warm smile as a little tear trickled slowly down her cheek.

"Well we can't risk the map being stolen any longer," said Gary breaking the silence. "We'd better go down to Kent as soon as possible and see if we can find that diamond for you, Miss Wilson; what do you think Rashid?"

"I agree. How about this weekend?"

"Fine by me," said Gary.

"Yes, the sooner the better," added Chris.

"Oh do be careful boys," said Miss Wilson looking up, "I don't want you to do anything dangerous."

"Don't worry Miss Wilson," I replied, "we're just going to have a look to see if the diamond is there. There's nothing dangerous about that."

Chapter 8

Spitfires and Skeletons

On Friday, after school, I was in the garden when Ahmed came out. His father was upstairs talking with Dad.

"*Assalamu Alaykum*, Rashid. How are you?" he said trying to make conversation.

"*Wa Alaykum Assalam*. I'm fine *al-hamdulillah*."

We shook hands.

"What's the problem between you and Huda?" I asked, getting straight to the point.

"Well... it is very difficult to explain," said Ahmed looking a bit embarrassed as he sat on the bench. "You see, in Islam a wife must respect her husband. This is very important." He hesitated. "It's just that I feel sometimes that Huda is not showing me enough respect."

I went over and sat next to him.

"But you can't get respect just by telling someone to respect you," I said choosing my words carefully. "Respect has to be earned by treating others with respect. The way you talk to them and act towards them, taking them into your confidence, or asking their opinion, that sort of thing."

Ahmed didn't respond. I think he was a bit surprised by what I said. I tried hard to think of something else sensible to say.

"Remember what the Prophet, peace be upon him, said? *'The best of you, is he who is best to his wife.'*"

Ahmed looked at me. Gradually a huge smile broke across his face. He stood up, pulled me to my feet, and gave me a warm hug.

"You are a good boy Rashid," he said as he tousled my hair. "Huda is lucky to have a brother like you."

I was tempted to say, 'I know!' but just then Mum called us in to eat. Dad and Ahmed's father were already sitting at the table along with my sisters and Kalim. As I started to eat Kalim looked at me.

"Did you say *Bismillah* before you started eating?" he asked. "If you don't say *Bismillah* then *Shaytan* is going to eat some of your food."

"Yes I did say *Bismillah,* thank you very much Sheikh Kalim!" I replied sarcastically. Since he had started saying all his prayers on time, he had started to think he was the resident expert on Islam. He went around telling everyone what they should and shouldn't do. To be honest I was beginning to find it very irritating.

"Well, I didn't hear you," he said taking a spoonful of food. "And make sure you eat with your right hand!" he demanded.

"Ha! That's funny coming from you," I laughed, "seeing that you don't even know which one is your right hand."

"Yes I do!" pouted Kalim as he held up his right hand. "This is my right hand," he declared, before holding up his left hand. "And this is my wrong hand."

Everyone laughed. But Kalim took no notice. Instead he just

looked across the table and saw Mum drinking some water.

"Take three sips first Mum, that's how the Prophet, peace be upon him, did it."

"Okay, that's it Kalim!" I said pushing my chair back. "Look, you shouldn't go around telling people what to do like that."

"Yes I should!" he protested. "Sohaib told me that in Islam we have to remind each other."

"Not like that Kalim. It's very rude!" I said angrily.

"Rashid is right Kalim," agreed Dad. "You must show respect to others."

Then Dad smiled.

"I'm glad you are trying hard to be a good Muslim, Kalim. But the best way to show others the right way, is by doing it yourself."

Kalim remained silent for the rest of the meal. At the end of the meal he leaned over to me and whispered, "There's something I don't understand Rashid."

"What's that Kalim?" I asked.

"There are many people who don't say *Bismillah* when they eat, right?" he said.

"Yes," I replied. "But what's your point?"

"Well, if *Shaytan* eats all those people's food, isn't he going to get sick?"

"Oh Kalim, you're so funny," I laughed. "I don't think it means he actually eats all their food!"

"You mean he leaves some?"

"Er... well I suppose so, I've never really thought about it," I said feeling a bit confused.

"Perhaps he leaves the vegetables," said Kalim, half to himself. "Nobody likes the vegetables."

The big day arrived; the day that we had arranged to go down to Kent to solve, at last, *insha' Allah,* the mystery of the Haupmann Diamond. I was so excited I couldn't get back to sleep after the *Fajr* prayer. I phoned Gary and Chris and we caught the early train from Waterloo to Harford Town, arriving just before 9am. A row of buses were waiting outside.

"Excuse me, do you pass through Fernham?" I asked one of the drivers as I leaned in through the open doors.

"Yes, hop on lads!" said the driver with a friendly smile.

The bus was empty and we relaxed at the back and watched the countryside pass by. We saw the ruins of an old castle on a hill in the distance as the road twisted and turned past farmland and cottages. Eventually we stopped at a small group of houses.

"Here we are lads!" said the driver, pointing to the houses.

"Is this it?" I asked in disbelief. "It doesn't look like a village, just a few old houses."

"You wanted Fernham village didn't you?"

"Yes, but…" we chorused.

"Well this is it, now come on lads, I can't wait all day."

The hydraulics hissed as the doors opened. We all jumped off and watched as the bus pulled away, leaving us in the tiny and very quiet village.

"Take a look at the map Rashid and see where we are," said Chris.

I put my hand in my top pocket to get the map out.

"Oh no!" I cried as I started searching through all my pockets, again and again in a panic, spilling out the contents onto the pavement. "Oh no! I can't find the map."

"Oh Rashid, you haven't lost it have you?" cried Chris anxiously.

"I don't know… I can't remember," I stammered.

"Keep your hair on guys, there's no need to panic," said Gary coolly pulling the map out of his pocket. "Never fear, Gary is here!" he said chuckling. "When we were over at your house the other day I was looking at some of your books and the map fell out of one of them," he said. "I took it with me. Sorry, I forgot to tell you."

"Al-hamdulillah!" I said feeling very relieved. "Now let's have a look at it."

We could see the village marked in the bottom left-hand corner, and a huge forest stretching out towards the north.

"Here, look!" said Gary. "There are some standing stones near where Michael Wilson's Spitfire went down on the edge of the forest. If we can find them, then it shouldn't be very hard to find the Spitfire."

"Perhaps we could ask someone," said Chris looking around.

But there was no one in sight. The village looked deserted. We decided to walk down the road in the hope of finding someone. A small post office was built into one of the few houses. As we opened the door, a little bell rang, and an old lady stepped out from a back room.

"Hello," she said peering over the rim of her glasses. "What can I do for you?"

"Hello," I smiled. "We were wondering where we could find the standing stones, marked on this map." And I held the map out for her to look at. But she didn't look at it.

"Ah yes, you mean the Pilgrims Crossing," she said, smiling at us. "We get quite a few ramblers round here visiting that place. You'll find it up on that ridge." She pointed up the road that we had just walked down.

"Follow the road out of the village and you should see a stile that will take you onto the footpath that leads straight up there."

"Thank you very much," I said politely and we left the post office and headed back up the hill.

It wasn't a very long walk, but because it was uphill, we made slow progress. Eventually we reached the group of standing stones, or the 'Pilgrims Crossing' as the old lady had called it, and decided to rest a while before going on.

"I wonder why it's called the Pilgrims Crossing?" I said as we sat down to rest on one of the fallen stones.

"I think it's because these stone circles were used like markers or signposts in ancient times and travellers used to pass through all the time," suggested Gary. "I saw a programme on the TV about it. They said if you look at a map of Britain you will see that all the stone circles line up in perfectly straight lines. They called them 'Ley Lines' and said they are like ancient roads."

"They must have been very clever to line up all the stones in a straight line over miles of country," said Chris, obviously not very convinced. "And how did they drag the stones up to these places? I thought people in ancient times were not as clever as we are today."

"I don't think that's true," I said. "Just because we have lots of technology now doesn't mean we are more intelligent."

"Yes," agreed Gary. "And just because our life is more complicated now doesn't mean it is any better either." He chuckled and we all joined in.

For a moment or so we said nothing and just sat there at the top of the hill, leaning back on the large stone slabs letting the summer sun gently warm our bodies. It was very peaceful and tranquil up there.

"Come on!" declared Chris suddenly as he sprang up and pointed down the hill to the forest below. "That must be where Michael Wilson's Spitfire crash landed."

Gary and I studied the map again.

"Yes, that seems to be the place," I said. "It should be right at the edge of the south west corner of the forest, which means it should be visible."

We skipped down the hill a lot faster than we had trudged up. "I don't understand why it was never found. I mean, after all these years, surely someone would have spotted something as big as a Spitfire," said Gary.

"Well it seems that those who reported seeing Michael's plane crash made a mistake," I said stumbling through the bracken. "Most of the sightings say it crashed into the sea, which is a couple of miles south from here, at least."

When we got to the spot marked on the map, we searched and searched, but found nothing.

"Are you sure this is the right place?" shouted Chris, feeling increasingly frustrated. "There's nothing here but stinging nettles and poison ivy!"

"I don't understand," I said feeling very confused, but trying to stay calm. "According to the map, it should be right here."

"Maybe the forest boundary has grown since the war," said Gary. "Perhaps we should start searching further into the forest," he suggested.

"Good idea Gary," I said and we went deeper into the forest, cutting through the undergrowth with our sticks.

"I'm going to climb up this tree to get a better look," said Chris.

"Can you see anything?" I asked when he was about half way up.

"Only trees and more trees," he said, sounding very disappointed.

After searching for almost an hour, we made our way back out to the edge of the forest where we had begun our search and sat down on some old logs that were covered in ivy.

"What a waste of time!" said Chris angrily. "We've come all this way, for nothing."

"Don't give up yet Chris," urged Gary. "We can try further down the line of trees. It must be around here somewhere."

"Did you remember to bring the sandwiches with you?" I asked Chris. "I'm starving after all this exercise."

"Me too," added Gary who came and sat next to me. Chris took the sandwiches from his bag and joined us.

"Shift up," he said, "so I can sit down too!"

"Be careful!" said Gary as Chris sat down beside us. "This log is beginning to wobble."

The log creaked, as if it was about to crack. I stood up and looked at it closely. It was completely covered in ivy and most of it seemed to be stuck in the ground. I pulled away some bits of overgrowth. As I did, I saw that the log was smooth underneath! I realized that it wasn't a log at all!

"Allahu Akbar!" I shouted as I started tearing away the ivy and weeds from around the log. "This isn't a log, it's the Spitfire!" I shouted excitedly. "It was right in front of us all the time, but we couldn't see it!"

I pulled away a large piece of ivy and there in front of us was the faded, but still recognizable, yellow, blue, white and red circles of the Royal Air Force insignia on the side of the fuselage.

"If this is the fuselage," I said tugging away more ivy, "then the cockpit is further down there." I pointed to where the 'log' went into the ground.

We set about clearing away over sixty years' worth of weeds and debris.

"Here's the canopy!" shouted Chris, and we all joined him pulling up nettles, bracken and ivy with our bare hands, ignoring stings and cuts.

Then, as I tore away a huge clump of weeds, I saw the white dome of a human skull in the open cockpit below us. We pulled away more debris then sat back and gazed in shocked silence. There, in front of us, was the complete skeleton of Miss Wilson's father, Michael, still sitting in the cockpit where he had died all those years ago. It looked like a scene out of a horror movie. His uniform had partly rotted away and his bones were bleached white. His jaw gaped with a twisted and grotesque smile and his long bony fingers were still clasping the side of the cockpit. He looked as though he was about to stand up, as though he had been waiting all these years for someone to come along and clear away all the overgrowth just so that he could climb out.

I was trembling and none of us could speak. As we sat on the grass, frozen by terror, a tall, thin man appeared from nowhere and ran over to the cockpit, where Michael's skeleton was sitting. It was Nick Grimes. With scant respect for the dead, he reached in and started searching the corpse.

"Hey, what are you doing!" shouted Chris as he stood up. "Get away from there!"

"Thanks for doing all the hard work for me, kids," laughed Grimes. "Now, where's that diamond?"

"Come on," shouted Chris, "we can't let him get away with this!"

But as Gary and I stood up, two large men grabbed our arms and dragged us out of the way.

"Hurry up Nick!" shouted the man with a gruff voice. "We can't hold these kids all day."

"It's not here!" rasped Grimes.

"What're you talking about?" asked the other man. "The diamond has to be there! You'd better not be trying to trick us…"

"Look I tell you it's NOT THERE!" said Grimes turning away angrily. "Look for yourself if you don't believe me!"

He grabbed me and squeezed my cheeks. "Where is it? Where is the diamond?"

"I don't know… it should be there!" I stammered.

"Come on Nick, let's get out of here before someone sees us and calls the cops!" said the gruff one nervously.

Nick Grimes pinched my cheeks hard.

"OK, we're going, but that diamond is mine. I've sacrificed too much to lose it now. I'm gonna be keeping a close eye on you."

He slapped my face and then signalled to the two men. All three disappeared into the forest as suddenly as they'd arrived.

"Huh! Those bullies don't scare me," said Chris jumping up and waving his fists in the air as if he wanted a fight.

We shook the dirt and grass from our clothes and headed back over to the Spitfire where Michael's skeleton had been pushed forward onto the dashboard by Grimes' rough hands.

"He said the diamond isn't there," said Gary peering cautiously into the cockpit. We took turns to search, as respectfully as we could in the circumstances. But Nick Grimes was right; the diamond wasn't there.

"At least we found the Spitfire and Michael's body," I said eventually. "Miss Wilson will be so happy that at last she can give her father a decent burial."

"Yes," agreed Chris, "I can't wait to see her face when we tell her."

"We'd better go back, or we'll miss the train from Harford Town," I said turning to walk back up the hill towards the stone circle.

"What about Michael and the Spitfire?" asked Chris, hesitating near the fuselage.

"We'll tell the police when we get back," I replied. "They'll take care of it."

As we walked I was deep in thought.

"What's the matter Rashid?"

"I don't know," I replied. "There is something not quite right about all of this, but I can't put my finger on it."

"Are you worried about Nick Grimes and his bullies?" asked Chris.

"No, they don't frighten me. It's the Spitfire. I mean how come it was so well hidden?"

"It crashed over sixty years ago Rashid," said Gary, "so it's not surprising that it got covered in undergrowth and ivy."

"Yes, but it wouldn't have got covered straight away," I said. "How come nobody spotted it?"

"That's a good question," said Gary, "but don't forget that it hit the ground at high speed and was partially buried. Not only that but it was right on the edge of a forest, with trees all around, so it wouldn't have been easy to spot."

"I suppose so," I responded, "but I get the feeling that someone made sure that nobody would find it. I think someone tried to hide it deliberately."

"You don't think Heinrich tried to hide it do you?" asked Chris.

"Why would he want to hide it?" I retorted. "It wouldn't make sense; I mean he wanted the plane to be found."

"I'm pretty sure it wasn't Heinrich," said Gary, looking puzzled, "but who was it? And why would they want to hide the Spitfire and Michael's body?"

"Perhaps whoever it was didn't want anyone to know that the diamond wasn't there any more," said Chris.

"Well we know it wasn't Heinrich, because he put the diamond in the cockpit with Michael so that it would be found," I said, thoughtfully. "And we know it wasn't Michael, because he is still sitting in the Spitfire where he died."

"Then who could it have been?" asked Chris.

"Didn't Flying Tiger mention an observer?" I asked. "He said that when Heinrich's bomber was shot down, both Heinrich and his observer bailed out but only Heinrich was captured. The observer was never found. Perhaps he has something to do with all of this."

"Perhaps," said Gary. "Perhaps."

We walked on in silence, each one trying to make some sense of this puzzle.

Chapter 9

The Observer

Almost a month had gone by since we had found the Spitfire. Miss Wilson had her father's remains brought back from Kent and buried at the local cemetery, next to her mother. She was so happy that we had found him and wasn't the slightest bit interested in the whereabouts of the diamond. So we just let things be for a while. But it was always in the back of our mind. "Thank you so much boys," she said as we sat in her house after the funeral. The head teacher had given us special permission to stay off school for the day.

"Mother will be so happy now that Father has come home," she smiled. "She changed after he disappeared, you know. She would become angry and shout at me, and told me I was a bad girl and thought that it was my fault that Father had gone away.

But it wasn't my fault, was it Rashid?" and she looked searchingly into my eyes.

"No, Miss Wilson, it wasn't your fault." I smiled, trying to comfort her.

"You're such a good boy, Rashid," she said as she patted me on the head.

"And Mother is not angry any more, now that Father has come home." At this, she began humming and straightening out the creases in her dress.

The next day Ahmed came round to go to the regular Friday evening programme at the mosque with Dad and me. Kalim, who was playing with Amir, came to the door.

"I want to go too!" he said, "I'm a big boy now!"

Dad smiled, "Okay Kalim, let's go!"

But as we left Amir started crying loudly.

"Can Amir come too?" asked Kalim. "He's a big boy as well."

"No," said Dad, gently but firmly. "He's too young."

Amir's screaming got louder and louder as we walked down the garden path. As we reached the gate, Huda came out of the house carrying a sobbing Amir.

"*Assalamu Alaykum!* I'll come with you, otherwise Amir just won't stop crying," she said. "He's become so attached to Kalim, *masha' Allah.*"

When we got to the mosque, Amir didn't want to go with Huda to the Ladies' Section; he wanted to stay with Kalim in the men's.

"It's okay," said Ahmed, "we'll take care of him." He smiled.

Amir followed Kalim as if his mum and dad didn't exist and sat down right next to him. He even copied the way Kalim sat cross-legged and folded his arms, and kept looking at him every now and again to check that he was copying exactly what he was doing. When Kalim laughed Amir laughed. When Kalim sneezed, Amir sneezed, or tried to. He even scratched his nose when Kalim scratched his nose.

The mosque was very full and the guest Imam had started his lecture, so we listened quietly. His topic was the importance of our intentions. He said that Allah will judge our actions by our intentions, by what is in our hearts. Because of the larger than usual crowd, he stood on the small wooden pulpit so that he could be both seen and heard. As I listened I noticed two tiny hands appear suddenly on the rail in front of the Imam. Then I saw a little head peeping over the top and looking out towards the congregation. My heart jumped; it was Amir! Somehow he had crawled off while we weren't looking and climbed up the steps to where the Imam was speaking. I looked around quickly for Kalim, in time to see him crawling towards the front, obviously following Amir. The Imam continued to talk and didn't give any indication that he was aware of the child standing there with him. In fact, amazingly, no one else appeared to have noticed either, not even Dad and Ahmed! I decided not to make a fuss, in case it made matters worse.

By this time Kalim had crawled up the steps to the pulpit and now his head also popped out above the rail in front of the Imam. I was trying hard not to burst out laughing. Now there were three people standing in the pulpit. The Imam giving the lecture, and Kalim and Amir poking their heads over the rail smiling at everyone in the mosque. After what seemed like ages, some people noticed and started to giggle. Eventually the Imam himself looked down theatrically to see two small children grinning up at him. He smiled a wonderfully warm smile and lifted Amir up into his arms.
"Oh my goodness!" cried Dad. "That's Amir!"
He glanced at the spot where Amir and Kalim had been sitting. Amir was laughing his head off and was clearly enjoying the whole thing. The Imam gave him a kiss and a cuddle then asked, "Do these two delightful children belong to anyone?"
I wondered which 'delightful' children he could be talking about. Dad stood up and slowly picked his way through the congregation sitting in tightly-packed rows on the floor. He

was blushing profusely by the time he reached the Imam and apologised to him. But the Imam just laughed and said, "It's really no problem; children are a joy and a blessing from Allah!"

Dad tucked the two children under his arms and began the long walk back. A buzz went around the hall as people stared at what was, after all, a fairly rare occurrence, even at the Friday evening programme. Noticing this, Kalim stared back at everyone and then shouted out, "Please pray for us everyone! Pray for us!"

That was enough to set the whole mosque roaring with laughter. Apart from Dad that is! When we got home and told Mum and the others, they all thought it was hilarious. Even Dad began to see the funny side of it. While we were talking, Kalim made a big turban for Amir and sat him on a chair.

"We have to call him Sheikh Amir now!" he declared, and we all laughed.

The following Saturday we went to the RAF Museum in Hendon with Miss Wilson. She had agreed to have her father's Spitfire put on display there and we were to be among the first visitors to have the opportunity to view it.

"It's in pretty good shape considering that it crash landed," said Miss Wilson as she stretched out her hand across the rope barrier and touched it gently.

"Yes," I agreed, "it is. They've done an excellent job of cleaning it up and restoring it. It hardly looks damaged at all."

"This one's a Heinkel," called Gary who had walked towards the other exhibits. "Just like the one Heinrich flew."

We joined him and stared up at the huge black bomber. It was a Heinkel *He 111* with a glass domed front, which meant you could see right into the cockpit, where the pilot and observer would have sat above the nose gunner.

"The crew members were a bit exposed weren't they?" said Chris walking around the front. "I mean, if a fighter plane approached from the front, they could shoot straight through all that glass; it wasn't much protection."

"Well they did have guns to defend themselves," I said. "Plus, of course, there were the fighter escorts."

I pointed to the small yellow-nosed fighter plane next to the bomber. "These fighters would fly just above the bombers, waiting for the British to attack and then they would dive in for the kill."

"That's just what happened to my father," said Miss Wilson poignantly. "These battles only lasted a few seconds and the pilots usually had very little time to think."

I looked around the museum. The aircraft were clean and polished, silent and empty. It was hard to imagine that these machines once screamed through the skies, guns blazing, bringing terror and destruction, death and sadness. Now they were museum pieces, historic curiosities, but the reality was that these planes were instruments of war and war was an evil thing. I wondered how Miss Wilson was feeling as she looked at the planes around her. They must have stirred terrible memories of the struggle to survive and the loss of her father. It was a loss that had affected her deeply. A loss she had never quite come to terms with.

"Shall we go for a cup of tea?" I asked, hoping to cheer her up.

"What a good idea Rashid," said Miss Wilson enthusiastically. "Museums always make me tired, hungry… and thirsty!"

"Me too Miss Wilson," I nodded with a smile.

We walked away from the aircraft and the memories of war and back to the present, a present where I live in peace; a present where I have my family and friends around me; a present where I am free to do what I want, thanks to the Grace of the Almighty and the sacrifices and suffering of people like Miss Wilson and her father.

When I got home, Mum asked me to keep an eye on Amir who was trotting up and down the garden path. He had recently learnt to run and was enjoying this new skill, which he still hadn't quite mastered! He would toddle for a few steps laughing his head off, then fall down flat on his face onto the soft grass. But he didn't mind, as long as he thought that nobody was watching him. If you were, then he would start to cry and hold his arms outstretched for you to pick him up and kiss "it" better. Sometimes "it" would be his hand; at other times it would be his arm or his knee. He would hold it out and whimper pathetically until you kissed it. This, of course, worked like magic, after which he would be up and off toddling down the garden again. The funny thing was, he would sometimes forget which hand he had actually hurt and give you the 'wrong' hand to kiss. It made me realize that we learn how to manipulate a situation to get attention at a very early age! But I couldn't blame the little fellow. All he wanted was a kiss and a cuddle. Sometimes I wish Mum would give me a kiss and a cuddle, the way she used to when I was little. Being grown up is not as much fun as people think.

Today Amir didn't see me watching him and so he just got up and toddled off, laughing wildly. When he got to the end of the garden, where tall bushes mark the border with the neighbour's garden, he stopped and looked through the fence. His face became serious and he stared intently through the holes in the wooden fence. He had reached the end of his world. This was it for the moment. What lay beyond that fence was unknown to him, but he loved to stare at it. It was mysterious and magical with new, strange creatures. Like the large Alsatian dog that stood chained to its kennel at the far end of the neighbour's property. Sometimes it would sit up and bark when Amir stretched his hand through the fence. At which point he would pull his hand back in quickly. But he wouldn't run away. His curiosity was stronger than his fear.

"Amir!" I called, and he turned round and came towards me. Then he began twirling around in a circle. Round and round he went with his arms outstretched.
"No, no, no, that's enough now or you'll start getting dizzy," I said, but he didn't care, in fact he wanted to get dizzy. He twirled

round and round until he wobbled and staggered and I had to catch him as he fell.

I laughed and shook my head.

"Time to go in Amir!" I said as I walked towards the kitchen door. "I think that's enough running about for today." Of course, he didn't want to go in and he squirmed about trying to get free, but I held tight.

"Tough luck mate, I'm stronger than you!"

Children never seem to listen to advice or warnings and don't learn until something happens to them. But I suppose we are all like that. Some of us only learn by making mistakes. Maybe that's why Allah put us on this earth, so that we learn the hard way through our own mistakes. Sometimes I wonder why He didn't just make us all good straightaway.

Once inside Nur told me that there was a telephone call for me:
"I think its Gary."

"Thanks," I said, handing Amir to her.

"Hi Rashid."

I recognized Gary's voice immediately.

"Do you fancy coming over to play some computer games with me?" he asked.

"Sure, I'll be over in 10 minutes."

After several games of Virtual Tennis, Virtual Soccer and Virtual Combat, I was virtually exhausted! And I had lost every single game to Gary, who was an expert at anything and everything to do with computers.

"Shall we look at the discussion boards at SimHQ.com?" he asked.

"We might as well. I don't think there's anything left for you to beat me at," I laughed.

Gary logged on to the web site and entered the general notice-board area. He showed me the various discussions, or 'threads', as he called them.

"Here's an interesting one about the latest game being developed," said Gary as he opened the thread.

Just then a bell chimed and a little window opened up on the screen.

"What's that?"

"It's a private chat window; you can make a list of all your friends and when they are online, you can chat to them," replied Gary.

"Have you put me on your list of friends?" I asked.

"Well I would, but you haven't got a computer at home, you Wally!"

"Oh yeah, right!" I laughed. "Who's this message from then?" I asked, leaning over Gary's shoulder.

"It's Flying Tiger! It says – Hi eagle, how R U? Need any more info WW2?"

I looked at Gary: "What's all that R and U stuff?"

"Oh those are abbreviations. When you chat or send text messages, you can shorten words to make it easier. So are becomes R and you becomes U and stuff like that."

"I see," I said, not really understanding why having code words would make it easier. "Why don't you ask him if he knows anything about Heinrich's observer, the one who bailed out but was never found?" I suggested.

"Good idea," said Gary. "It's worth a try."

"Hello Flying Tiger, I'm fine. Actually do you think you can find any more info on Heinrich's observer for me?"

The words appeared almost instantly, as did the reply.

"Will do my best cya."

"What's C-Y-A?"

"It's short for 'see you'," said Gary. "You get used to all this jargon when you use the Internet as much as I do."

A few days later, while we were walking home from school, Gary showed us an e-mail he had received from Flying Tiger. Chris and I listened intently as he read it out.

"Hi Eagle, the observer's name was Franz Uber. He had been

91

Heinrich's observer for a year. Witnesses say he bailed out safely but no one knows where he landed or what happened to him after that. Sorry Eagle, that's all I could find. Happy hunting! FT."

"Well that doesn't really help us does it?" said Chris, sounding very disappointed.

"Be positive; at least we know his name was Franz Uber," said Gary, trying to sound positive himself.

"Perhaps we know a bit more than that," I said with one of my 'be quiet, I'm thinking' looks.

"What do you mean?" he asked.

"Well if there is no record of him, then that means he was never captured or found dead."

"OK, but how does that help us?" asked Chris.

"It means he was around when Michael's plane crash landed," I continued, "and he must have known about the diamond, because he was Heinrich's observer for a year."

"Are you suggesting that this guy, Franz Uber, took the diamond?" asked Gary, stunned by the simplicity of my line of thinking.

"Perhaps he did," I replied. "Perhaps he landed in the forest and was hiding when he saw Heinrich put the diamond in Michael's plane. Perhaps he then stole it once Heinrich had gone."

"Well that would explain why the diamond wasn't there when we found the Spitfire," said Chris, catching on slowly.

"Yes, and it would explain why the plane was hidden," I went on. "Franz Uber wouldn't have wanted Heinrich to know that the diamond wasn't where he'd left it. If Michael's Spitfire had been found, Heinrich would have heard about it, realized that the diamond hadn't been found, and then alerted the authorities that Uber was still alive – with the diamond, don't forget – so that they could go to search for him."

"Do you think he's still alive?" asked Chris.

"Who knows?" I replied. "But I suppose we have to keep an open mind."

Chapter 10

A Cave by the Sea

"Are you going anywhere special for the Easter holidays?" asked Gary as the bell went and we filed out of school on the last day of term.

"Well my Dad promised to take us to that theme park… what's it called again?"

"Alton Towers."

"That's the one. But apart from that we haven't really got anything planned."

"Why don't we go back down to Kent?" suggested Chris. "There may be some clues we overlooked last time."

"Well it is the last place that Franz Uber was seen, as he bailed out of his plane," I said, warming to the idea. "If we are going to try to find him, then that would be as good a place as any to start."

We all agreed; at least it would give us something to do over the next two weeks.

When I got home I found Ahmed sitting in the living room. We greeted each other with *Salams* and I sat next to him on the sofa.

"How are things?" I asked.

"Fine, *Al-hamdulillah,*" he answered. "Huda's coming back home with me today, *insha' Allah.*" He said this with a broad smile on his face.

"Masha' Allah, that's great news," I smiled. "Has everything been sorted out between you two then?"

"Yes; *insha' Allah* things will be much better now," he said. "Life is always full of problems Rashid, that's why it is a test for us. I've realized that the solutions are not always simple. But if we are patient and understanding towards others, then Allah will help us."

I nodded in agreement: "Allah is always on the side of those who are patient."

Huda came downstairs holding Amir in her arms.

"Assalamu Alaykum. I'm going to miss that little chap," I said getting up to give Amir a kiss.

"Are you ready to go now Huda?" asked Ahmed.

"Yes," replied Huda with a smile, and handing him the baby.

"Can I come with you?" asked Kalim who was upset that his little playmate Amir was leaving him. "I can be your baby too! You can have two babies!"

"I'm sorry Kalim, you have to stay here," said Huda. "But don't worry; you will be able to see Amir plenty of times, *insha' Allah,* when you come round or when Ahmed and I come to visit."

"Are you in love again?" asked Kalim innocently, looking at Ahmed and Huda.

Ahmed laughed, and he blushed a little as he did so.

"Yes, Kalim," chuckled Huda. "Is that alright with you?"

"Yes, that's fine by me," he smiled. "And are you going to be nice to each other now?"

"Yes!" smiled Ahmed, now well and truly embarrassed and heading for the door.

"Well that's okay then," said Kalim. "So now you can have more babies, *insha' Allah.*"

"Er… that's enough from you Kalim," I said putting my hand over his mouth, much to Ahmed's relief. And Huda's too if the look on her face was anything to go by.

As they drove away I could see Amir in the back crying for Kalim.

"Babies are cute," said Kalim looking thoughtful and with his hands on his hips. "But they are such hard work."

"Well you should know Kalim," I laughed, and started tickling him and chasing him round the house.

A few days later I went with Gary and Chris to retrace our steps to Fernham. It wasn't long before we were back at the spot where the Spitfire had crashed. Of course it wasn't there any more and the whole area looked as if it had been ploughed up and then flattened by heavy vehicles. There wasn't much to look at now so we walked back up the hill towards the Pilgrims Crossing.

"You can see the coast from here," said Chris jumping up on to a huge boulder and pointing into the distance.

Gary climbed up next to him and shaded his eyes as he looked out towards the sea.

"If Franz Uber had been here, then he may have tried to get to the coast," he said, thinking out loud. "He would probably have tried to find a boat or something so that he could get back to Germany."

"Well according to my Ordnance Survey map," I said hoisting myself up on to the boulder next to them, "there is a footpath that runs across farm land here, hugging the hedges by the sides of the fields all the way to the coast. It would have been perfect cover for someone trying hard not to be seen. Most of these old paths have been public rights of way for centuries, so it would have been there during the war. If he did try to get to the sea, he would probably have gone that way."

"Well what are we waiting for, let's go!" said Chris jumping down from our vantage point. "We can't come all this way and not go to the seaside!" he laughed.

The sun shone brightly as we raced down the hill and followed the footpath south to the waiting coastline, which came into view after an hour's steady trek across the fields.

"Look at that!" cried Chris excitedly, pointing to the huge white cliffs that dropped straight down to the sea.

"Do we have to get down there?" I asked, feeling decidedly anxious.

"We have to if we want to cover every possibility," said Chris. "There must be a way down, surely."

We looked along the cliff top in both directions.

"And there it is, over there!" he said, pointing to an iron stairway just visible a little way to our right.

As we got nearer we could see a heavy chain barring the way. Above it there was a sign, saying: "Danger High Tide! – No Admittance."

Chris walked to the edge and looked down.

"The water's miles away!" he scoffed. "There's no danger, come on, let's go under the chain and climb down!"

I hesitated, wondering if we were going to get into trouble.

"Come on, Rashid!" urged Gary. "We can climb back up long before the tide comes in."

"Alright, but just a quick look." And we ducked under the chain one by one.

We followed the steps down as they wound round the contours of the cliff until we reached the beach below. It was completely deserted, possibly because there were signs all over the place, warning of the dangers of being stranded by the tide.

We searched around the beach for any clues that might have told us if Franz Uber had been there all those years ago. But all we found were countless seashells, dead starfish, and debris washed up by the tide.

"Come on there's nothing here; let's get back up the cliff, before the tide moves any closer," said Chris as we walked along the beach.

I looked up at the huge cliffs towering above us and saw that there were a few small caves dotted here and there.

"You know, he would probably have tried to hide in one of those caves, especially if he was caught by the tide," I said pointing up the cliff walls. "And there wouldn't have been all these warning notices in wartime!"

"That's funny," said Gary looking up as well. "I didn't notice the caves before, but you're right, let's go and take a look."

We scrambled across the pebbles and sand. When we reached the foot of the cliffs we climbed up onto some huge boulders and then pulled ourselves up into the first cave entrance. It smelt damp and stale and it was very dark. Gary lowered his small rucksack onto the floor of the cave.

"It's a good job that one of us has the brains to think about bringing a few things with him," he chuckled as he pulled out a torch and shone it around the cave.

"Hey look at this!" shouted Chris excitedly. His voice echoed around us.

He lifted up a large rock, revealing what looked like a very old and rusty gun. I picked it up carefully and Chris let the rock fall back down with a crash.

"It's very old, definitely from WW2," I said. "Just the sort of pistol a German pilot might carry."

"It must be Franz Uber's!" cried Chris. "That means he was here! In this cave! Amazing!"

We all looked around with a growing sense of excitement.

"He probably sat right here with his gun in his hand," said Gary, "looking out onto the beach below, to see if anyone was following him."

"Then he must have hidden it under this rock," I added.

"But why? I mean, why did he leave it here?" asked Chris.

"Maybe this was just his lookout post," suggested Gary, "and he went further inside the cave to hide."

We all turned and peered anxiously through the darkness of the cave. Gary shone the torch further down into the gloom. The walls were damp and water was running down in some places. There were a few rocks and boulders on each side, but the cave was very deep and disappeared beyond the light of the torch.

"We didn't come all this way to stop now," said Gary. "Come on, let's go deeper."

Just then, we heard some rocks falling outside the cave entrance.

"What's that?" cried Chris. "Is someone there?"

We all stopped still for a moment and listened, but there was nothing to hear except the sound of the waves breaking gently on the beach below.

I went to the mouth of the cave and looked around outside, but didn't see anything unusual.

"Nothing here," I reported.

"Don't worry Chris, it was probably a seagull flying off a ledge and loosening some rocks or something," said Gary trying to allay our fears. "It's nothing to worry about, come on, let's go!"

We huddled close together as we walked slowly and nervously deeper into the cave, following the dim light from Gary's torch. Every now and then Chris glanced back, as if he sensed that there was someone, or something, following us.

As we walked the cave became narrower and lower and we found ourselves walking in single file, with our heads bowed low. Finally we had to stop when we reached what looked like a dead end.

"We can't go any further," said Chris. "Perhaps we'd better turn back."

"Hang on a minute," said Gary who was crouching down low and shining his torch through a small hole near the floor of the cave. "The cave gets bigger past here, if only we can squeeze through." And he lay flat on the ground and began to crawl through the hole.

"Hey it's massive through here!" called Gary, who was already half way through the hole. "Come on, it's easy to get through!" And he wriggled the rest of his body through and disappeared from view entirely. Now that he had gone, his torchlight had gone too and it was very dark. I couldn't even see Chris, even though he was standing right beside me.

"Hey Gary, shine that torch back through here will you?" I shouted. "We can't see a thing!" But there was no reply.

"Chris, are you there?" I said holding out my hand to see if I could touch him.

"Yes right here Rashid!" he said with a slight tremble in his voice from somewhere very close to me. "You know I'm not sure that this is such a good idea. Perhaps we ought to be getting back."

I was about to reply when we heard a sound in the darkness behind us. It sounded like footsteps. Then it stopped.

"Did you hear that?" whispered Chris. "There's somebody behind us!"

"Come on Chris, let's get through the hole quick."

I grabbed him and guided him to where I thought the hole was; it was completely dark and we couldn't see a thing, but I was right about the hole. I pushed him through. When I felt his legs disappear I got down onto my stomach and squeezed myself through, spurred on by the terrifying thought that someone was going to grab my legs and drag me back.

When I dragged myself up on the other side I could see Gary quite a way off, shining his torch around. Chris was standing just next to me and he helped me to my feet.

"Gary was right, this place is MASSIVE!" he said in amazement.

The ceiling of the cave was so far above us that the light from Gary's torch could barely reach it. There were stalactites hanging over us and stalagmites protruding from the ground, parts of which fell away into the bottomless darkness below. From the faint sound of splashing, I guessed that it must be the sea down there, but it was too gloomy to see anything. Gary shone the torch in our faces as he came running over.

"Hey guys, what do you think? This place is pretty neat eh?"

"What's the big idea going off and leaving us like that Gary?" I said reproachfully. "We were left in complete darkness!"

"Oh sorry Rashid, I didn't realize. This place just took me by surprise."

"Shine your torch back over to the hole," said Chris. "We heard footsteps behind us."

Gary shone the torch towards the hole, but everything seemed still and quiet, apart from the occasional drip… drip… drip… of water from the stalactites.

"Are you sure you heard footsteps and not water dripping?" said Gary. "You know when people get scared they imagine all sorts of things."

"No we didn't imagine it," said Chris indignantly. "It was definitely footsteps, wasn't it Rashid?"

"Er,… I think so," I said, not really sure myself.

"Well who do you think it is?" asked Gary.

"Perhaps it's Franz Uber," replied Chris.

"It can't be Franz Uber," I retorted, "he can't still be down here after 60 years… can he?"

"I once heard that they found this old Japanese soldier from the Second World War who was still hiding on an island in the Pacific," said Gary. "It took them a long time to convince him that the war had ended."

"Look, there's no way that it can be Franz Uber," I repeated. "He couldn't possibly have survived down here all that time. He would have had no food or warmth and would have died in no time."

"Perhaps it's his ghost!" said Chris.

"Of course it's not a ghost," I said looking to Gary for support, but he just shrugged his shoulders.

"Who knows? The way I feel right now I could believe anything."

"Well, I think you are being silly. If there is anyone following us, then it is more likely to be Nick Grimes and his crew," I said adamantly.

"Oh thanks Rashid, that makes me feel much better," said Chris sarcastically.

"Come on you two, there's no point in standing here getting cold, let's go on and see what we can find," said Gary, and he walked away across the cave.

Chris and I hurried after him, staying close together. Every now and then we would hear something in the distance, a rock falling, or a gust of wind, or the crash of water far down below. Each time we would stop and look around nervously. Although I hated to admit it, I also had the feeling we were not alone. Was it Nick Grimes as I had suggested? Or was it Franz Uber still hiding out in these caves after all these years? Or, as Chris thought, his ghostly spirit, roaming the caves where he died? Or, worse still, was it something else? When I was little, Dad had told me stories about the *Jinn,* which had fantastic powers. They liked to hide in caves and could take many shapes and forms. When my father had told me these stories, they seemed like amusing fairytales. But now, in the darkness, they preyed on my mind and seemed very real. I read *Sura Al-Falaq* and *Sura An-Nas* from the Qur'an to myself – and silently questioned the wisdom of parents who tell their children about such things!

We continued through the cave in silence, each one of us deep in thought, haunted by fears and doubts. Trying bravely to suppress our fears, we pressed on, getting deeper and deeper into the darkness.

Chapter 11

Dead Man's Trap

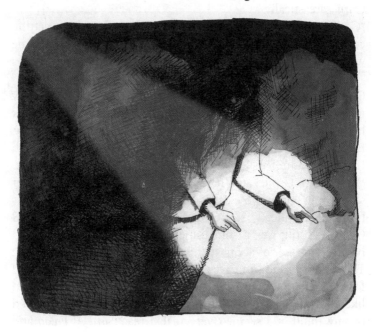

Finally we reached the edge of a giant chasm where we had to stop. There was only one way across. A thin neck of stone that jutted out towards the other side, but fell a little short, leaving a gap of about 2 metres for us to jump, in order to get to the other side.

"It's only a small jump," said Gary, "we can do it easily!"

"Do you think the ground will hold our weight?" asked Chris stepping tentatively on to it with one foot.

"It's solid rock," said Gary, "of course it's safe."

"Listen!" I said. "Can you hear something down there?"

We all peered down into the darkness below and listened to the faint sound. It was a sort of 'whooshing' sound.

"Must be the sea," said Chris as he dropped a stone down.

It disappeared into the darkness and took ages to make a tiny splash as it hit the water far below.

"I'm still not sure about that rock," said Chris. "I mean, if it breaks, we're going to fall all the way down there!"

The thought of falling all the way down there began to make me feel nervous too.

"Look it's not too late to go back, you know," I said.

"We can't go back now," pleaded Gary, "we've come too far to stop now."

"Okay," I said, "but it wouldn't be a bad idea to hold on to each other as we go across."

We all held hands and shuffled slowly across in single file. As I walked my eyes peered down into the darkness below and I began to feel dizzy.

"Don't look down!" whispered Gary behind me.

Those few steps seemed to take an age. Finally we leapt, one by one, on to the other side. It was such a wonderful feeling as we tumbled onto the solid ground. We turned around and looked back across the chasm.

"There you are," said Gary, "I told you it was solid as a rock!"

But as he spoke there was a loud crack and the neck of rock we had just walked across suddenly went crashing down into the darkness.

Chris gasped in horror: "That could have been us!"

"And now there's no way back," I added, "now we really have no choice but to go on."

"Well at least no one can follow us," said Gary.

"You mean no one living can follow us!" corrected Chris.

We went on in silence. Gary's torch was beginning to fade and only lit up a small area around our bodies. Beyond that was total darkness. There was an eerie silence apart from the strange 'whooshing' sound that seemed to echo all around. We hadn't really planned on walking so far and our shoes did not have thick soles, so all the sharp stones were beginning to make our feet very sore. But we kept on walking until we reached what seemed like a dead end. We walked around and around but there didn't seem to be any way through the cave walls, which were different in this part of the cave. They weren't solid rock like before, but piles and piles of boulders, as though there had been a massive rock fall and everything had just landed in a haphazard sort of way.

"I'm exhausted!" complained Gary as he sat down on the dusty floor.

"Yes me too and I'm starving," added Chris as he collapsed beside him.

"So, did either of you Brain Boxes bring anything to eat?" he asked.

"Or drink, I'm really thirsty," I said as I joined them on the floor.

As I sat down on one boulder it began to shake. Suddenly it seemed that all the boulders around me were shaking and trembling but before I even had time to shout out a warning to Gary and Chris the floor beneath my feet started to give way. The next thing I knew I was being sucked down into the ground in a cloud of dust and rubble. A split second later I hit solid ground again with a bump. As the dust settled I realized Gary and Chris had fallen through with me into a larger cave. My back was sore as I pulled sharp rocks out from under me. A stale and musty smell filled the air and it took a few moments for us to stop coughing and choking.

"Is everyone okay?" I asked as I fumbled around in the darkness.

"My leg hurts," answered Chris, "but I think I'll live."

"Just a few cuts and bruises I think," said Gary as he picked up his torch and slowly shone it around the cave, lighting up the jagged walls.

"Look over there!" shouted Chris.

Gary shone the torch straight ahead. We all gasped with fear at the sight before us.

Sitting quietly in the corner of the cave was a man in uniform leaning back against the wall. His eyes were closed as if he was asleep. We just stared, not daring to move.

"That must be him! Franz Uber!" I whispered as if I was trying not to wake him.

"Is he dead or sleeping?" asked Chris.

"Surely he must be dead," I said, getting up slowly and creeping cautiously over to the body. As I got closer I could see his face much clearer. It reminded me of the mummified bodies I had seen at the British Museum. It was dry and wrinkled like a prune.

"He's dead alright, come and have a look," I said beckoning to Gary and Chris. "It's amazing how his body has been almost perfectly preserved!"

Gary leaned over and studied the body carefully.

"You're right, he is incredibly well preserved. He must have got sealed in here by a rock fall that made it airtight, which explains why his body hasn't decayed at all."

"Then that must be how he died," I added. "I mean, if this cave was airtight then he would have suffocated."

"Do you think he has the diamond on him?" asked Chris.

"Well, I suppose one of us will have to search him," I said, sounding braver than I felt.

"Not me, I'm not going near him," insisted Chris.

"And I'd rather not touch him either," added Gary as they both backed away.

"That's not fair, you can't do that," I protested as I walked nearer to Franz's last resting place.

"How about we draw lots?" I said as I started to look around on the ground for something to use. But Gary and Chris didn't reply.

"Okay you guys, let's toss a coin. Has anyone got some change on them?" But they still didn't answer.

"Hey guys," I said, raising my voice, "are you deaf?"

I turned to where they were standing and to my horror I saw

Nick Grimes instead, holding Gary's torch.

"No need to flip a coin Rashid," he said with a crooked smirk on his face, "I'll search our friend Franz Uber for you."

I could see Gary and Chris behind him, being tied up by the two thugs.

"Let my friends go!" I shouted as I ran over to Chris and Gary, but the three men grabbed me and pulled my hands behind my back. I felt the rope tighten around my wrists and I was shoved onto the floor next to Gary and Chris.

"Are you two okay," I asked.

"Yeah, we're okay," said Chris.

"Sorry we couldn't warn you Rashid," said Gary. "They had their hands over our mouths."

"Don't worry lads," chuckled Grimes, "once I have the diamond and am safely away, I'll phone the police to come and get you. After all I don't want to hurt anyone. I'm just after the diamond. Talking of which, I think it's time to search our German friend here."

He bent down and began searching through Franz Uber's pockets and the pile of old clothes that was next to him. Then he searched the area around him. He started to become angry and frustrated.

"Come over here you two and give me a hand!" he shouted and the two men went over and started searching with him.

"What about his hands?" said the one with the gruff voice.

"There's nothing there, I checked already!" snapped Grimes.

"No, I mean he seems to be pointing. Both hands are pointing in the same direction."

"You're right!"

Grimes stood up and shone the torch in the direction Franz was pointing.

"Our very dead friend is trying to tell us something," he said.

"He's trying to tell us that the diamond is over there."

He peered carefully through a gap in the boulders.

"Yes! There it is! I can see it! It's just behind these rocks. How considerate of old Franz," he laughed, "pointing to the diamond for us with his last dying breath. Very considerate indeed!"

He began to laugh so loud that the echoes around the cave walls caused a few stones to fall down.

"Come on you fools, I'm not paying you just to stand there! Come and give me a hand to shift these boulders, so I can reach the diamond."

The two men ran over and began to push the rocks and boulders out of the way. As they did so the rocks began to shake. Suddenly, the wall began to collapse.

"Quick, it's going to collapse. Get out!" shrieked Grimes as the whole side of the cave came tumbling down. But his warning was too late. When the dust settled, all we could see was Grime's crooked arm sticking out beneath a huge pile of boulders. All three men had been completely crushed.

It had all happened very quickly and now everything was still and silent. We had thrown ourselves onto our sides during the rock fall, and for a while we were too shocked to move or even speak. Eventually I pulled myself upright and shuffled over to where Franz Uber was still sitting. I swivelled around until my hands could reach inside his pocket.

"I saw Nick Grimes pull out a knife from in here. Let's see… ahh yes, here it is!"

I pulled out an old and rusty camping knife and carefully rubbed the blade against the ropes still tying my hands. It took some time to cut through, but once I had freed myself I went over to Gary and Chris and freed them as well.

We walked back over to where Grimes and his men had been crushed by the rock fall. I had never seen someone die before. It made me feel sick and numb at the same time. We just stood there staring at his outstretched hand. It was pale and still, as if he wanted us to pull him out of the rubble.

"It was a trap," I said, breaking the silence. "Franz Uber

planned this! He knew he was going to die, so he threw the diamond behind those boulders knowing that if anyone tried to get it, they would have to loosen some of the rocks, which would make the whole thing collapse."

"That's why he was pointing to it," added Gary, "so that whoever found him would think he was showing them where the diamond was. But it was really a trap!"

"I suppose he thought that if he couldn't have the diamond, then no one could have it!" said Chris.

I looked at Franz Uber, who was still sitting peacefully up against the wall of the cave. Even in death he had managed to play one last trick. And now he sat there, with a sardonic grin on his face. I could almost hear his grotesque laughter echoing around us.

Standing there I noticed there was a gentle breeze blowing into the cave. It hadn't been there before. I looked around. The rock fall had opened up another passageway and in the distance I could see a thin shaft of light piercing the darkness. It was sunlight.

"Look at that," I said. "If there's sunlight, then there must be a way out."

"Come on," said Gary. "Let's get out of here before any more rocks start falling, I don't want to spend another minute down here."

"Hang on a minute," I said picking up something that had caught my eye amongst the rocks, "guess what I've found."

I held up a huge diamond.

"The Haupmann Diamond! YES! At last we found it!" cried Gary.

"I'm not sure if I'm glad or not," said Chris. "I mean it's supposed to be a lucky diamond, but so far it doesn't seem to have brought anything but misery and death! Perhaps we should just leave it here."

"A stone can't bring misery or death, any more than it can bring luck," replied Gary. "It's just a stone. What happens to you depends on what you do and not some shiny stone!"

"That's absolutely right," I added. "What happened to Franz and Nick Grimes had nothing to do with the diamond, but had everything to do with them. It was the greed in their heart and their evil intentions. If your intention is evil, then only evil will come of it. But our intention is not evil. Our intention is good. It is to help someone who deserves help."

"Okay, okay!" said Chris anxiously. "I get it. We're the good guys. Now let's get out of here before we become the dead guys!"

I popped the diamond in my pocket and we scrambled quickly over the rocks and boulders. We followed the tunnel until we reached the sunlight. Chris cupped his hands so that Gary and I could climb up onto the ledge over our heads. Then we turned and pulled Chris up too before scrambling along the ledge and squeezing through a small gap into the bright sunshine. We sat on the grass for a while until our eyes got used to the light, and then we looked around to see where we were.

It was a little gorge, not far from the white cliffs we had walked down to get to the beach so after a short rest we walked back up to the top of the cliffs and down towards the road a short way off. There weren't many cars on the road, but we managed to flag one down and ask the driver to take us to the nearest police station. After lengthy explanations there we were taken home in the back of a plush police car with a motorcycle escort.

I had already phoned Mum from the police station and she had invited Miss Wilson over by the time we got back. We didn't waste any time in telling her the good news and we gave her the diamond, which the police had confirmed was now rightfully hers.

"So this is the famous Haupmann Diamond," she said as she

held it up to the light. It sparkled and glittered. "I've never seen such a thing in all my life!"

Then she looked at me and smiled.

"Do you think it will go well with my white dress Rashid?"

"Oh yes, Miss Wilson, you'll look beautiful!" we all laughed together.

"Now you can buy your house from the council," I said.

"And they can't put you in a Nursing Home," added Chris.

"Oh thank you so much boys, it is such a relief," she smiled. "But I'm just glad you are safe and sound and no harm came to you."

I suppose it was when Miss Wilson tried to pay for her council house with the Haupmann Diamond that someone told the newspapers. Once the story got out, it was mayhem. We had radio and television crews camped outside our door wanting to interview us and the telephone would not stop ringing with all sorts of offers for the diamond. We agreed that we should only do an interview with Miss Wilson present. She turned up in one of her favourite white dresses, covered with sparkling white sequins and lace.

"It goes perfectly with the diamond," she smiled.

The local newspaper splashed the story across the centre pages and we even made the BBC nightly news. But the best part was when we went back to school. As we entered the gates all the pupils and staff made two lines for us to walk through, clapping us all the way to the school doors. We even got a standing ovation at assembly where the head teacher told everyone what we had done. He then called us up onto the stage to collect the school's 'Award for Service to the Community'.

I felt good, really good inside as I realized that it wasn't about the diamond at all. It was about friendship and it was about helping others. That had always been our intention and, "Actions are judged by their intentions!"